MYTH LEGENDS

VOLUME 1: THE SEARCH FOR

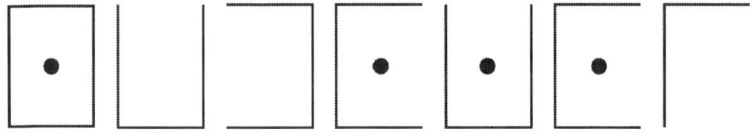

IANDSBOU UINDNUZY

Myths and Legends
Volume 1

Copyright © 2019 by Turn Around Enterprises, Inc.

All rights reserved. This book or parts thereof may not be reproduced in any form, stored in any retrieval system, or transmitted in any form by any means—electronic, mechanical, photocopy, recording, or otherwise—without prior written permission of the publisher, except as provided by United States of America copyright law. For permission requests, write to the publisher, at the address below.

Printed in the United States of America

First Printing, 2019

Written by Brooklynn Hoffmann
Cover Designed by Nathan Hoffmann

Trade Paperback ISBN: 9781732713543

Turn Around Enterprises, Inc.
PO Box 351695
Palm Coast, FL 32135

https://puzzlepause.com
https://mythsandlegendsbook.com
https://facebook.com/initiationbook

PuzzlePause

ACKNOWLEDGMENTS

This book would not have been possible without the generous help of so many people.

First, I would like to thank Tida, Jennifer Priester, Gerco Korteweg, Adrian Clabburn, Brent Thompson, Michael Gherna, Jesse, Jason, Anne, Jo Ellen and the other 209 backers who supported this project on Kickstarter. Your support validated this idea and helped bring it to life.

Next I would like to thank my awesome beta tester Valerie for reading through the stories and providing me with great feedback.

Thank you Dad for always guiding me through every step and challenging me to create the best product it can be. Thank you Mom for creating the puzzles and helping me format the book - you're a life saver! And it wouldn't be complete without my sister Chloe' for helping me brainstorm and write these stories.

I couldn't have done it without any of you.

Thank you to all those who have purchased this book. I hope you all enjoy this as much as I do!

- Brooklynn Hoffmann

WELCOME

This is a book about stories. Stories are powerful. They shape culture, belief, tradition, and provide a way to explain the unexplainable. They move us to action and create a framework for us to communicate and share understanding.

Some stories survive. Myths and Legends is about these stories. No one really knows how they began. They may have some truth, be based on experience, or just be carefully crafted ways to impress or persuade. Either way they have become part of a living history.

Myths and Legends are unique because they are passed from one generation to the next. As they weave through time they change. Like in the telephone game each generation leaves their mark, but they take on a life of their own.

The Myths and Legends in this book are not the original stories. They are my personal interpretations. This is another step in that evolution.

I selected ten stories that all have a central purpose. They provide answers. But their value is in more than just an answer.

As you learn more about these stories think about how they are connected. The relationship is printed in symbols on the front cover of this book. By the end you will know what it is.

PUZZLE STORIES

This book contains ten myths and legends from around the world in the form of puzzle stories.

At the beginning of each chapter is a story. Important words have been removed. Your objective is to fill in the blanks by solving puzzles. Pay close attention to the puzzle instructions page. Once you have the missing words you will have to guess how they complete the story.

Each story ends with a question that you can answer. Use all of the information we have given you. Once you have figured out the answer to the question you are ready to move on to the next story.

I selected stories from around the world. In Myths and Legends you will find stories from Greek and Norse traditions, Africa, Asia, Scotland, Canada, and the United States. Some may be familiar. Others may not. Just like the storytellers of old, our hope is to broaden your horizons.

While these are not the full stories, you will have enough details to continue the search on your own. I encourage you to explore the stories even more.

Let the journey begin!

- Brooklynn Hoffmann

THE CODEX

Need help solving some of the puzzles? Get the Codex! Thanks to the generous support of our Kickstarter friends we have created a special document to guide you through the puzzles. Each puzzle with a hint has a black circle next to it with a number like this: ①

All you have to do is find that number in the Codex to get the hint. Some of these hints have multiple parts to them and the Codex will direct you to another number if you need more help.
The Codex is FREE and can be downloaded here:

www.mythsandlegendsbook.com/book1codex

THE VAULT

Would you like to see the answer key?

The Codex will give you everything you need to solve these puzzles but it will not provide the final answers. If you need an answer to a specific puzzle, or want to check if you got the story right, go to:

www.mythsandlegendsbook.com/book1vault

The Vault is free to access and use. Just register on the website and enjoy. Now you have everything you need to begin. Good luck!

THE STORIES

The Lost City 1

The Hunt 12

Close Encounter 26

The Ghost 41

The Storyteller 55

The Bargain 68

True Form 83

Pots and Pans 97

The Trickster 110

The Goddess 124

THE LOST CITY

Just moments ago everything was normal. The streets were quiet and peaceful. The market was closing for the day and everyone was returning home. I was waiting to meet someone. I could see a group of young children laughing and dancing without a care in the world.

They are no longer there.

What is happening?

The sky is dark. The air is thick and heavy. The sound is deafening. The mountain is throwing rocks down on us and the ground is shaking so violently I cannot stand.

Stone streets are splitting in half. Men are shouting. Women are screaming. Infants are wailing. Beside me, I hear a desperate prayer to the gods but there is no answer. Where is _____ now that we need him? Can he not hear our cries?

The statue of King _____ has fallen. The temple is gone.

How could the gods do this? They created our city, our nation, our people. Because of them we are mighty, rich, and powerful. Our borders stretch across _____ and _____, as far as _____ and _____.

We waged war on _____ and struck terror into the hearts of the _____. How could the gods be angry with us?

What have we done?

It's all happening so fast. I see nothing but ruins.

THE LOST CITY

Buildings are engulfed in flames and bodies now litter the streets.

My family is down there somewhere and I cannot move. I cannot do anything but watch.

Is there nothing we can do? Does everything have to be destroyed?

Are we so evil that we didn't deserve a warning?

I never believed this would happen. All our might, our strength, our power - where is it now?

The mountain is crumbling around me but I cannot bear to see it. I close my eyes and breathe in the dusty air.

I am waiting to die.

Where do I live? _____

Write the clues from the puzzles in the spaces below. Complete the story by figuring out where the clues fit in the story.

Story Clues:

_____
_____
_____
_____
_____
_____

PUZZLE INSTRUCTIONS

Puzzle 1: Framework

Complete the framework puzzle and write down the 20 letters in the circled boxes. Unscramble the letters into three words. The words will be used to help you solve Puzzle 2.

Hint: The first word is six letters and begins with "H". The second is 11 letters and begins with "E". The third is 3 letters and begins with "S".

These 3 letters are three of the 20 found in the puzzle.

Puzzle 2: Cryptogram

Solve the cryptogram to decode a question. This puzzle is missing three words. Put the three words from Puzzle 1 into the phrase to answer the question and get the story clue.

Puzzle 3: Cryptogram

Puzzle 3 has three different cryptograms. They all use the same alphabet. Solve each one to reveal a three part clue that will help you find a story clue.

Puzzle 4: Word Search

Use the word bank at the bottom of the page to find the words in the puzzle. There are 5 intersecting letters in this puzzle. Write down the intersecting letters and unscramble for a story clue.

PUZZLE INSTRUCTIONS

Puzzle 5: Codebreaker

Each letter has a numerical value. You have been given two letters to start. Use the given letters and find their numbers in the puzzle to fill in the alphabet key. Once you have the alphabet key, use it to decode the story clue at the bottom of the puzzle.

Puzzle 6: Word Maze

Your starting point is the circled letter. Use the words at the bottom of the page to find and mark them in the puzzle. Unlike word searches, the letters are not all in a straight line. These words can go up, down, forward, and backward.

As you solve the maze, the trail will double back on itself 2 times. Collect the 4 words that intersect and write them down as the story clues.

Need a hint? Get the Codex:
www.mythsandlegendsbook.com/book1codex

THE LOST CITY

Puzzle 1: Framework 32

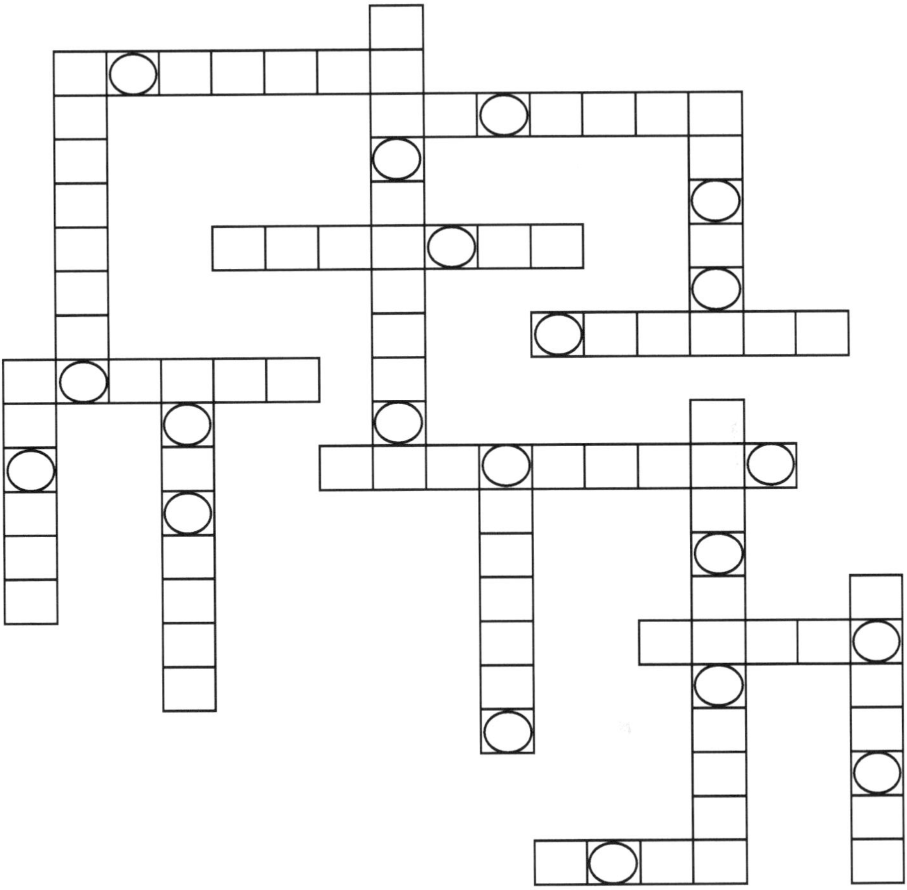

4 LETTERS
ROME

5 LETTERS
GENOA

6 LETTERS
ASSISI
URBINO
VENICE
VERONA

7 LETTERS
BAMBERG
CASERTA
FERRARA
POMPEII
RAVENNA

8 LETTERS
FLORENCE
ISTANBUL

9 LETTERS
DUBROVNIK

11 LETTERS
CINQUE TERRE
MACHU PICCHU

Write the 20 letters on the previous page to unscramble the 3 words. Place the answers below.

42 H__________

70 E________________

169 S_______

THE LOST CITY

Puzzle 2: Cryptogram 98

ZL   DLSZOLH   JZNHPFG,

APIN   BOFO   WLPBL   MPF

UDLG   IZMMOFOLH   HJZLAN.

HJOG   SFODHOI   DLZUDYN,

RYDSON,   DLI   BDHSJOI

PEOF   UDLWZLI.   HJZN   API

BDN   WLPBL   DN   HJO

SFODHPF   PM   _____   DLI

HJO   API   PM

_____   DLI   HJO   _____.

(Remember to put the three words from Puzzle 1 into the empty spaces. It will help you solve it.)

WHO IS THE PERSON REFERENCED IN THIS PUZZLE?

_____

This is the first story clue. Write it on page 2.

Reminder: You can check your answers in the Vault at:
www.mythsandlegendsbook.com/book1vault

THE LOST CITY

Puzzle 3: Cryptogram 24

1. W T P   X N U W T J M O D P   V Y
   Z P E W P U K   D N L N M N S O W N V K .

2. D V K W U O U I   W V   J V J H M O U
   X P M N P Y ,   W T P   O K D N P K W
   V M I R J N D E   Z P U P   K V W
   T P M C   T P U P .

3. P L N C P K D P   E H B B P E W E   W T O W
   W T N E   J M O D P   T O E   X P P K
   N K T O X N W P C   E N K D P   W T P
   K P V M N W T N D   J P U N V C   O K C
   Z O E   V D D H J N P C   N K   W T P
   P O U M I   O K C   R N C C M P
   X U V K S P   O B P E .

WHAT PLACE IS REFERENCED IN THESE CLUES?

_____

This is the second story clue. Write it on page 2.

THE LOST CITY

Puzzle 4: Word Search

```
L O G R Y Q Y L L Y N G K S A D I N O E L P M
J J A K B A R B R I S A W S P G S E N E M C N
N G Y N O M O L O S U C R D V E P G Z F Y O A
A Q T H A K H E N A T E N M E B F J K R W F J
C N I S K Q B F M I S W Y K E P A F U B Q O A
X A J N A O R E N T U M Y N Y R M S C X M Z R
S I S J S S F V D U G C V L O U Q L Q O N N T
A R U U E H V F W C U U A V Q G S V T U E I Q
E D B A I W I C Y A A X K Z P E R D M H O D M
F A L T F D T H M H I M O L G D E A Y L U M E
R H J H S A U X U C F V H V S D H P S H E N R
B B D Y Y H H A W A F B S L E K O S M N Z H N
A E R J Y R Q K L P N V A X N S H H K H X U E
A C U U O V X S W C E G E A E I I A V W E P P
V I X S E S S E M A R V T B V X U O I G R T T
W R P H Z D E Z O K H U H A P R M E Q P X W A
J A K G U F K R E H T O J M E S R P V B E L H
A L E X A N D E R N P I L Y N V C J Y P S L S
Y A F N A H K I A L B U K P E T O H N E M A K
Q I K J R I G N A H A J C O N S T A N T I N E
```

AKBAR
AKHENATEN
ALARIC
ALEXANDER
AMENHOTEP
ASHOKA
AUGUSTUS
CLAUDIUS
CONSTANTINE
CYRUS
DJOSER
HADRIAN
JAHANGIR
KHAFA
KUBLAI KHAN
LEONIDAS
MENES
MENKAURE
MERNEPTAH
NARMER
NERO
PACHACUTI
QIN SHI HUANG
RAMESSES
SARGON
SHIVAJI
SOLOMON
TRAJAN
TUTANKHAMUN
XERXES

THE LOST CITY

Puzzle 5: Codebreaker 67

	P												
1	2	3	4	5	6	7	8	9	10	11	12	13	14

					U					
15	16	17	18	19	20	21	22	23	24	25	26

__22__ __3__ __15__ __15__ __1__ __25__

THE LOST CITY

Puzzle 6: Word Maze

```
F G A L S S I A I N D I A J A P C E R
D P U E U D E B D Y O K L R D A S X E
B O M L R A W G R U M K A S U N L O R
W N B F O Y R J K E F T Y D L A E W O
S Q H R C S T Y C A N A D N R F S U K
I L T S C F W L A V U F A W O R U E C
Z R S Y O R O M T P Y G E N P I W E J
H I M B A B W E I A X R T L E C O C E
O Z L R D E Y U J M I A R T W A Y E M
H E Y R K I L O B M G T J Y A G R E R
Y C R H Y U J K L L E S T S L L O R S
L N T E J C V N E B B U E H E V E F I
M A O L O P R A C S A G R T S E A G H
U R T A N D A U S T R A S E P Y K R U
B F M L A S T N T J E D S K A Y P T D
C T H I O K L E R R C A U L K E Y R B
N U R L H N S T A F E M B O I P I F E
Y R G U A O A I L K R N A T S N E R K
```

1. COUNTRY KNOWN AS THE HEXAGON
2. AFRICAN NATION
3. NICKNAME IS "BEL PAESE"
4. HAS MORE LAKES THAN ANY OTHER COUNTRY
5. HOME OF PHILAE ISLAND
6. RABAT IS THE CAPITAL
7. LARGEST COUNTRY IN EUROPE
8. SEVENTH LARGEST COUNTRY BY TOTAL AREA
9. HOME TO ANCIENT WARRIORS THAT USED KATANA
10. HOME TO THE LARGEST LAND ANIMAL
11. OFFICIAL NAME IS HELLENIC REPUBLIC
12. CONTINENT NAMED AFTER A PRINCESS
13. CONTAINS MORE CASTLES PER SQUARE MILE THAN ANY OTHER COUNTRY
14. BECAME INDEPENDENT IN 1947
15. HOME TO THE TSINGY FOREST
16. WHERE COPERNICUS WAS BORN
17. HOSTED THE 1956 SUMMER OLYMPICS

PUZZLE WORKSHEET

What four words intersect in the Word Maze?

_____   _____

_____   _____

This is the end of the puzzles for The Lost City. Use this space to write down clues, unscramble words, take notes, and figure out how the missing words fit into the story.

THE HUNT

It is coming.

Soon the hunt will be over and our enemies and their pitiful creations will finally be destroyed.

My father, the great _____ _____, gave me a glorious purpose that I must fulfill: to hunt down _____ and _____ and forever destroy the _____.

We must move faster.

We get closer with every day that passes and soon we will break the curse. Once the _____ are gone everyone will know that the end has begun. We will release our father from his terrible prison and his power will be unleashed upon the _____.

_____ is looking back again. Locked in a course she cannot change, she holds a shield to protect the _____ _____ from the _____'s destructive power. She knows I am close.

I can smell her fear.

Just when I am about to overtake her the _____ hides again and I scream in anger. She may slip out of my reach for now, but tomorrow I will be back.

I hear a _____ in the distance. My brother's chase has begun. He hunts _____, keeper of the lesser _____. Maybe he will have more luck today.

I am exhausted but I can't close my eyes. This may be the night he wins. I eagerly watch and wait for the spell to be broken and dream of the day when we hunt together and rid the universe of _____ and _____ forever.

THE HUNT

My untameable rage and hatred fuel us. My brother's utter repulsion and mockery propel us forward.

Before everything there was _____, and _____ will reign again.

What are the siblings' names?

_____

_____

Write the clues from the puzzles in the spaces below. Complete the story by figuring out where the clues fit in the story.

Story Clues:

_____
_____
_____
_____
_____
_____
_____
_____

PUZZLE INSTRUCTIONS

Puzzle 7: Codebreaker

Each letter has a numerical value. You have been given two letters to start. Use the given letters and find their numbers in the puzzle to fill in the alphabet key. Once you have the alphabet key, use it to decode the two story clues at the bottom of the puzzle.

Puzzle 8: Codebreaker

Same as Puzzle 7.

Puzzle 9: Word Search

Use the word bank at the bottom of the page to find the words in the puzzle. There are 4 intersecting letters in this puzzle. Write down the intersecting letters and unscramble for a story clue.

Puzzle 10: Framework

Use the word bank to solve the puzzle. There are 10 circled letters in this puzzle. Once you have collected all the letters, unscramble them to get your story clue.

Puzzle 11: Word Maze

Your starting point is the circled letter. Use the words at the bottom of the page to find and mark them in the puzzle. Unlike word searches, the letters are not all in a straight line. These words can go up, down, forward, and backward.

As you solve the maze, the trail will double back

PUZZLE INSTRUCTIONS

on itself 10 times. Collect those intersecting letters and unscramble them for the story clue.

Puzzle 12: Crossword

There are a series of Across and Down clues you need to solve. There are 8 circled letters in the puzzle. Collect the letters and unscramble the word. The word is a story clue.

Puzzle 13: Cryptogram

Solve the cryptogram to decode a phrase. Once you have decoded the phrase, answer the question at the bottom of the puzzle for the story clue.

Puzzle 14: Framework

Use the word bank to solve the puzzle. There are 4 circled letters in this puzzle. Once you have collected all the letters, unscramble them to get your story clue.

Puzzle 15: Codebreaker

Same as Puzzle 7.

THE HUNT

Puzzle 7: Codebreaker

Clue 1

___ ___ ___ ___ ___ ___
 6   4   13   20   24   20

Clue 2

___ ___ ___ ___ ___ ___
 7   24   18   5   26   8

THE HUNT

Puzzle 8: Codebreaker 59

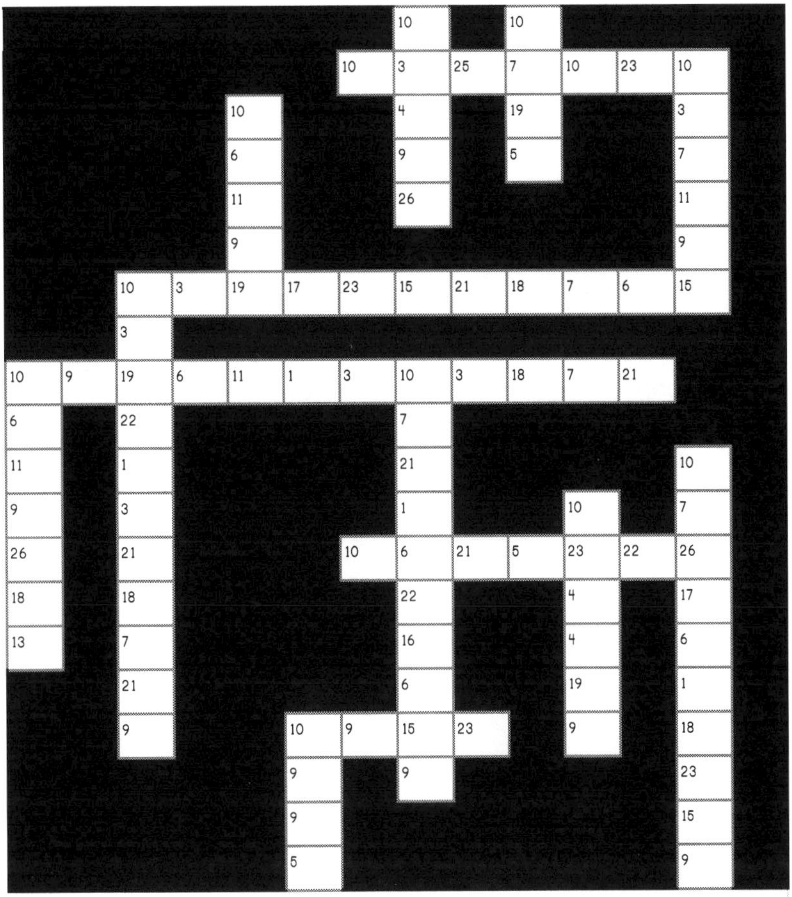

					O			E					
1	2	3	4	5	6	7	8	9	10	11	12	13	14

15	16	17	18	19	20	21	22	23	24	25	26

___ 10 ___ 3 ___ 15 ___ 7

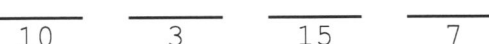

THE HUNT

Puzzle 9: Word Search

```
V U E K Z V O O K W O L S P S E I R A U T S E
L A I R T S E R R E T U N J S P R A I R I E L
T Z Z L E M M L Z E O D I R A I M E S F N C L
B R A L O P A Z K U S A V A N N A T R B R A U
X C C V E C K E D Y E U V Q Y Q F E W T E F L
S L I U I I X I N E T Y T B T P S U W R T J A
X C E P O K C V M S R A N F F H J Y O U Y C T
L Q O I F E V T E N I I D W W J W B C Q O N N
K R L N D Z V R A G F I A A I E J T I R R G E
T S S N I F O U A J M R T V W D T A A H R R N
L U T E U F V H T U N E Q B D Z E L Q Y T A I
A A E M N M E D H Z R E V R E V R P S S S S T
R D W I X P U R S L D N Y R F E W I S E P S N
R D A H M Y A U O U N S Q Z E J Y N R M S L O
A R N I E R K M C U D C X F X J I E E O Y A C
P M S Z D R H C T E S R F O R E S T X I M N B
A H D N D E S E R T I U O W A K H C N B N D S
H E U S Y J Q Z N V E B Y V C L I M A T E J S
C T I J E T A R E P M E T H E N I R A M E Z V
L P C I T A U Q A A N H B B E G F P U O F E V
```

ALPINE
AQUATIC
BIOMES
BOREAL
CHAPARRAL
CLIMATE
CONIFEROUS
CONTINENTAL
CORAL REEF
DECIDUOUS

DESERT
DRY
ESTUARIES
FOREST
FRESHWATER
GRASSLAND
HUMID
MARINE
POLAR
PRAIRIE

RAINFOREST
SAVANNA
SCRUB
SEMIARID
TAIGA
TEMPERATE
TERRESTRIAL
TROPICAL
TUNDRA
WET

___ ___ ___ ___

THE HUNT

Puzzle 10: Framework (11)

7 LETTERS
GAN EDEN
ELYSIUM
ZERZURA
HAWAIKI

8 LETTERS
TLALOCAN
TIR NA NOG
EL DORADO
SAGUENAY

9 LETTERS
FOLKVANGR
COCKAIGNE

10 LETTERS
OTHERWORLD
THEMYSCIRA
BRAHMAPURA

11 LETTERS
PANDEMONIUM

12 LETTERS
FIELDS OF AARU

___ ___ ___ ___ ___   ___ ___ ___ ___

THE HUNT

Puzzle 11: Word Maze

```
N U N E M M I B E Y D M R E P E L A H
S T S M A L L A O M F A N E P M E G X
O F E L I T T L E B I G I N H A L E E
L Q U J L E R S Y U M E T T Z C E U T
D O R E N H E Y L L P O V J E S A B S
N U O G O Y Y Y R A R O Y E O D Y M E E
A S F N N G D Y I D Z B S W D R L N N
U T F A K E R E A K C C Y N N D A E T
L U A D E F A S L L D L S U U B C D P
O O D N E Y D R T D U O K P S I Y N R
S N I A G A R O F Y O R K W I N D E E
T I B E S P S I L D B A D Y J V O I S
R I G H T L E F T A D D S U B T L R E
O H D L B C E R R S U T G J U R E F N
T J R O W B R O A D I H S T O A R E T
N A R C L K A S I B N G I L T C Y D E
C D M O C T S E W R I G H T E N F A N
E R E G O U C C T S A E T I X E R E T
```

1. RIGHT
2. LEFT
3. ADD
4. SUBTRACT
5. LIGHT
6. DARK
7. WINDY
8. CALM
9. ABSENT
10. PRESENT
11. ENTER
12. EXIT
13. EAST
14. WEST
15. COME
16. GO
17. COLD
18. HOT
19. NARROW
20. BROAD
21. BRIGHTEN
22. FADE
23. FRIEND
24. ENEMY
25. DOWN
26. UP
27. SUNNY
28. CLOUDY
29. FOR
30. AGAINST
31. IN
32. OUT
33. FAKE
34. REAL
35. SAFE
36. DANGEROUS
37. FOUND
38. LOST
39. SMALL
40. IMMENSE
41. LITTLE
42. BIG
43. INHALE
44. EXHALE
45. PERMANENT
46. TEMPORARY

___ ___ ___ ___ ___

___ ___ ___

THE HUNT

Puzzle 12: Crossword

ACROSS
1. A SIGNATURE
2. ATTRIBUTION OF A PERSONAL NATURE OR HUMAN CHARACTERISTIC TO SOMETHING NONHUMAN
3. WRITTEN COMMUNICATION
4. BOOK OF WORDS

DOWN
1. SET OF LETTERS
2. SHORT STORY THAT TEACHES A MORAL
3. MECHANICAL MACHINE FOR WRITING CHARACTERS
4. AN ACCOUNT IN WRITING OR THE LIKE PRESERVING THE MEMORY OR KNOWLEDGE OF FACTS OR EVENTS
5. INTERRUPTION OF CHRONOLOGICAL ORDER
6. THE CHOICE AND USE OF WORDS AND PHRASES IN SPEECH OR WRITING
7. USED WITH A PEN
8. CONTRAST BETWEEN EXPECTATIONS AND REALITY

THE HUNT

Puzzle 13: Cryptogram 114

```
XCN    JWA'L    NGP    XCNS
MWLJO    LC    EPPD    LOP    LTFP
OPSP.    W    KWX    CA    LOP
DYWAPL    FWSG    TG    YCAVPS
LOWA    CA    PWSLO.
GJTPALTGLG    NGP    WACLOPS
AWFP    LC    KPGJSTZP    CAP
KWX    CA    FWSG.    MOWL    TG    TL?
```

_____

THE HUNT

Puzzle 14: Framework 47

3 LETTERS
GEB
SHU

4 LETTERS
BABI
BAST
ISIS

5 LETTERS
FORUS
SATET
SOBEK

6 LETTERS
ANUBIS
KHONSU
NEKBET
OSIRIS
SERQET
TEFNUT
WADJET

7 LETTERS
IMENTET
TAWARET

8 LETTERS
NEPHTHYS

___ ___ ___ ___

THE HUNT

Puzzle 15: Codebreaker 133

PUZZLE WORKSHEET

This is the end of the puzzles for The Hunt. Use this space to write down clues, unscramble words, take notes, and figure out how the missing words fit into the story.

CLOSE ENCOUNTER

At first, I was skeptical but now I'm not so sure. After doing all this research, it seems absurd to just disregard it. I guess it all boils down to one question.

Do you really want to know if we're alone?

For the sake of privacy, I've attached three case files with missing details. There is a question at the end of each case that will give you what you need if you want to do more research.

I understand your hesitation regarding the subject but hear me out.

Sincerely,

Christine

Case Number 1: 1961

An _____ _____ and his wife were returning home from a weekend getaway to Niagara Falls when the unthinkable happened.

They were just a few miles away from a small town named _____ _____ in _____ _____ when they saw a bright white light behind them. The light followed them for several miles before the husband stopped to investigate.

As he walked to the forest, he claimed to see 8 to 11 humanoid creatures step out of a foreign aircraft and walk toward him. He ran to alert his wife but lost consciousness before he reached her.

CLOSE ENCOUNTER

The couple woke up several hours later with no memories of what happened. After a few months, the wife started having vivid dreams saying they were abducted and experimented on. These memories only fully resurfaced during hypnosis.

Since that night, nothing else has happened to the couple but both were firm believers and spoke often about the experience.

Case Number 2: 1989

At 3:15 AM a woman woke up from sleep to find five short creatures standing around her bed. Paralyzed and unable to speak, she was somehow levitated out of her apartment window in _____ and into a spaceship. The startling image was reported to local police stations from 23 independent witnesses.

A couple years after the incident, the woman reached out to a Ufologist and investigator by the name of ____ _____ after coming across one of his books. After hearing her story, he was determined to make sure it was properly documented.

During his research he received a letter from two men who identified themselves as "Richard and Dan" saying that they had seen the woman floating in the sky with three creatures toward an aircraft. They claimed to be bodyguards to a special political figure and wanted to meet with the woman to hear the rest of her story.

After some prodding, the investigator was led to believe that this political figure could be _____ _____ ___ _____ but that is strictly speculation.

CLOSE ENCOUNTER

The woman was advised not to speak with the men for concern that it would contaminate the story.

Case Number 3: 2001

Late one October night in _____, a woman named Petra woke up to the sound of shattered glass. She rushed to the living room to see a bright blue rectangular light that suddenly disappeared. A couple hours before, Petra's friend was lying on the couch watching the television. Now she was gone.

Petra's horrified scream alerted her friend's husband, Keith. He reportedly did not believe Petra at first and searched the entire property for his wife but she was nowhere to be found. Determined that it was some kind of alien abduction, Keith called the police department.

The _____ police department answered the call and were skeptical but they sent a few officers to investigate. After three hours with nothing to go on but a broken window and one mysteriously burned bush, Keith got a phone call from an unknown number.

The voice on the other end belonged to a doctor from a hospital in _____ which was nearly 500 miles away. He told Keith that his wife was dehydrated and frightened, but otherwise physically fine.

Police are still baffled by this mysterious disappearance.

How could she have possibly traveled that far in such a short amount of time?

CLOSE ENCOUNTER

29

What are these individuals' names?

Case 1: _____

Case 2: _____

Case 3: _____

Write the clues from the puzzles in the spaces below. Complete the story by figuring out where the clues fit in the story.

Story Clues:

_____
_____
_____
_____
_____
_____
_____
_____

PUZZLE INSTRUCTIONS

Puzzle 16: Framework

Use the word bank to solve the puzzle. There are 7 circled letters in this puzzle. Once you have collected all the letters, unscramble them to get your story clue.

Puzzle 17: Word Search

Use the word bank at the bottom of the page to find the words in the puzzle. There are 10 intersecting letters in this puzzle. Write down the intersecting letters and unscramble for a story clue.

Puzzle 18: Cryptogram

Solve the cryptogram to decode a phrase. Once you have decoded the phrase, answer the question at the bottom of the puzzle for the story clue.

Puzzle 19: Word Search

Use the word bank at the bottom of the page to find the words in the puzzle. There are 9 intersecting letters in this puzzle. Write down the intersecting letters and unscramble for a story clue.

Puzzle 20: Codebreaker

Each letter has a numerical value. You have been given two letters to start. Use the given letters and find their numbers in the puzzle to fill in the alphabet key. Once you have the alphabet key, use it to decode the story clue at the bottom of the puzzle.

PUZZLE INSTRUCTIONS

Puzzle 21: Crossword

There are a series of Across and Down clues you need to solve. The clues will give you the word you need to put in the puzzle. There are 10 circled letters in the puzzle. Collect the letters and unscramble.

Puzzle 22: Framework

Use the word bank to solve the puzzle. There are 11 circled letters in this puzzle with a number near them. Put that number on the corresponding line at the bottom of the page to find the story clue.

Puzzle 23: Codebreaker

Same as puzzle 20.

CLOSE ENCOUNTER

Puzzle 16: Framework

4 LETTERS
ECHO
GOLF
KILO
LIMA
ZULU

5 LETTERS
ALPHA
BRAVO
DELTA
OSCAR
ROMEO
TANGO

6 LETTERS
JULIET
QUEBEC
SIERRA
VICTOR
YANKEE

7 LETTERS
CHARLIE
FOXTROT
UNIFORM
WHISKEY

8 LETTERS
NOVEMBER

CLOSE ENCOUNTER

Puzzle 17: Word Search

```
O P B E A C H H A V E N Q S S U B M U L O C L
Q R W H I C P W O K O O R B Y A S D L O P E Z
C H T O L A A D C O K Y K I N H I U J I W C M
Q E T R E M D H O T V E N D U K C X P E N I A
G N B C O U A D T M L N N U K T X B S Q E T L
T G D U C P A X N I P A A N P R X U O W W S R
Z K H W L K H R E E L N M P E V S R Q M T Y C
B C O Z N S Q C Q S D D O Z P B V Y E Z O M N
K I T T E R Y X I H U M N T E I U J O N W H O
U R E U Z F Q A F W G L A Z S J Q N X M N Y T
K E U I T W I Y E P R B Z C L O U Z K L W R N
S D E L V L M N R X D A W T T O B W E P F B U
K E Q S E V A A Q L L I H E U L B S S X O I A
C R C M K U H V B L Z R H B H Q R I M D H R T
O F A Q K G R A M J A M E S T O W N D E I I T
N P D L V P U R Y B J V O L A K J N Q X A T P
C P I J I M D R D T Y B E E I S L A N D L I I
O R A N G E L E Y T A M O L Q Y L Y W B E S M
R R B Y A M E P A C O L A F F U B H F C A C G
D R O F M A T S O D B O G U N Q U I T P H K G
```

AMELIA ISLAND	DUXBURY	LUBEC
BEACH HAVEN	FREDERICK	MYSTIC
BLUE HILL	HARWICH PORT	NAVARRE
BOSTON	HIALEAH	NEWTOWN
BUFFALO	HYANNIS	OGUNQUIT
CAMDEN	ITHACA	OLD SAYBROOK
CAPE MAY	JAMESTOWN	RANGELEY
COLUMBUS	KENNEBUNKPORT	STAMFORD
CONCORD	KITTERY	TAUNTON
DURHAM	LEWES	TYBEE ISLAND

CLOSE ENCOUNTER

Puzzle 18: Cryptogram 146

M U Y X   M G   T O Y B   U J   M E X   I R L

R J P   M L R Z X Q   M G   R   J X A

H M R M X .   V O M   V X W G L X   F G O

D G ,   F G O   Y O H M   Z U H U M   M E X

G Q P   Y R J   G W   M E X

Y G O J M R U J .

_____

CLOSE ENCOUNTER

Puzzle 19: Word Search

```
S U T R S Y W V U U L L A B R E K C U R C G G
Z T M I K S A N F O R D M K U L S R X C E S M
B N A A W E Z Q J O R D A N H A R E P J N E O
E O E P W P T Y S N E K Q K A I W R L Z T Q G
L T T W L N E K U M I N U T E M A I D L U T H
L R J F E E C M H D A E M Y X U W U I J R L K
C E R W Y R S P D K Z Y M Z M I H F W D Y U R
E D G Z V G A A L N M L V H E D E M E B L M A
N A T V F U Y P E U U A F X T A V O M G I E P
T M R R O E E Y I P O N W Y C T U B B J N V E
R E N N F A L O F F N D D M Q S E A L X K K L
E Q Y E S D G I U N P A W A E O F F E T S Y O
S F D T W E I Y A E M W X U E I K E Y R E L I
S E G Z R Y R A E Z A G P M V H V Z Q A E E R
X I A E E C W J B K C Z D O R O W R A T K F O
Y Q G D L I L A M D L Q X O E V E O V S N I T
K I L K R A P Y A W N E F M V V M X R D A E W
T A R G E T U G L E X C K N A B S U I R Y L Z
O F N N O I G E L H H Z Q S E E S K N I A D T
B Y G S D R A Y N E D M A C B R O S E B O W L
```

ARROWHEAD
AZTEC
BEAVER
BELL CENTRE
CAMDEN YARDS
CAMP NOU
CENUTRY LINK
FEDEX
FENWAY PARK
JORDAN-HARE
KYLE FIELD
LAMBEAU
LEGION
METLIFE
MINUTE MAID
NEW ERA
NEYLAND
NOTRE DAME
OHIO STADIUM
ORIOLE PARK
ROSE BOWL
RUCKER BALL
SANFORD
STAPLES
TARGET
TIGER
US BANK
WEMBLEY
WRIGLEY
YANKEE

CLOSE ENCOUNTER

Puzzle 20: Codebreaker 78

											L		
1	2	3	4	5	6	7	8	9	10	11	12	13	14

								A			
15	16	17	18	19	20	21	22	23	24	25	26

_ _ _ _ _ _   _ _ _ _ _
9 23 25 6 22 2   17 22 2 22 26

_ _   _ _ _ _ _ _ _
20 22   8 4 22 12 12 23 2

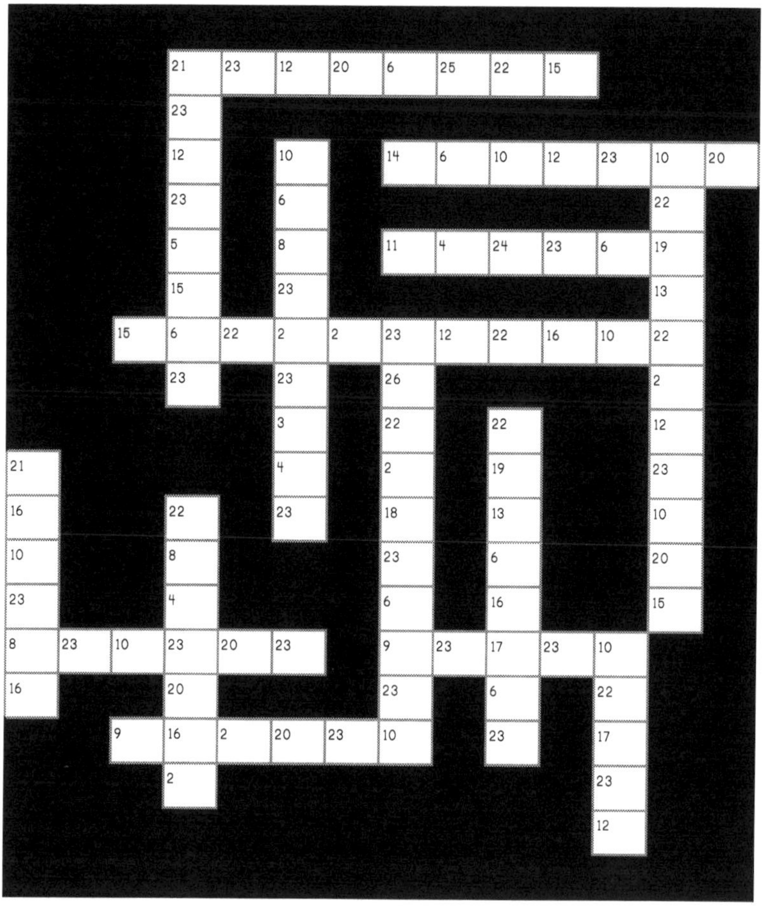

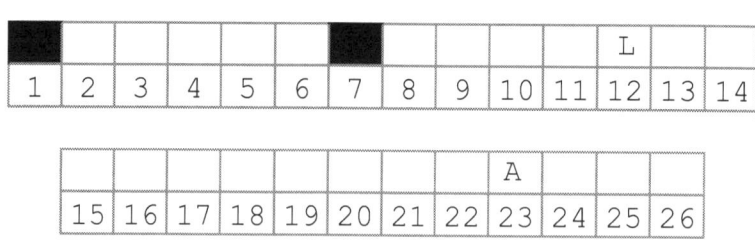

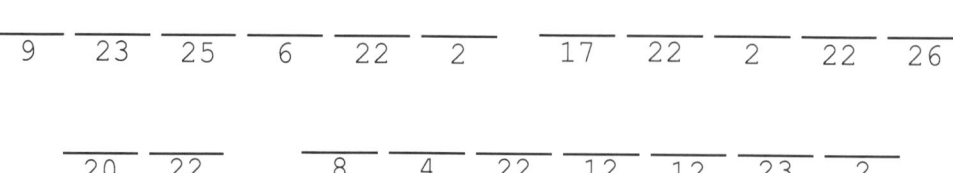

CLOSE ENCOUNTER

Puzzle 21: Crossword

ACROSS
1. ALCOHOLIC DRINK
2. FOOD SPREAD FROM YEAST
3. ELECTRONIC DEVICE FOR THE EAR
4. EXTENSION BLOCK; POWER BOARD
5. SMALL MACROPOD THAT TAKES SELFIES

DOWN
1. ON THE GRILL
2. SOUND FREQUENCY USED IN THE MEDICAL FIELD
3. ELECTRONIC RECORDING DEVICE ON AN AIRPLANE
4. SMALL PAD TO WRITE ON
5. ROTARY CLOTHES LINE
6. FLIGHTLESS BIRD
7. FACILITY ALLOWING USE OF THE INTERNET
8. WORLD'S LARGEST CORAL REEF

CLOSE ENCOUNTER

Puzzle 22: Framework

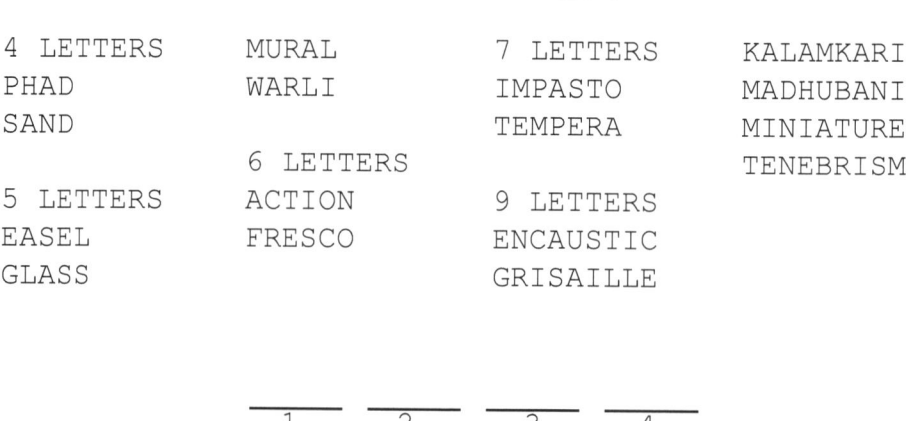

4 LETTERS	MURAL	7 LETTERS	KALAMKARI
PHAD	WARLI	IMPASTO	MADHUBANI
SAND		TEMPERA	MINIATURE
	6 LETTERS		TENEBRISM
5 LETTERS	ACTION	9 LETTERS	
EASEL	FRESCO	ENCAUSTIC	
GLASS		GRISAILLE	

___ ___ ___ ___
 1   2   3   4

___ ___ ___ ___ ___ ___ ___
 5   6   7   8   9   10   11

CLOSE ENCOUNTER

Puzzle 23: Codebreaker 41

PUZZLE WORKSHEET

This is the end of the puzzles for Close Encounter. Use this space to write down clues, unscramble words, take notes, and figure out how the missing words fit into the story.

THE GHOST

41

The sun was setting deep in the woods of _____.

The campsites were full. The tents were up. All around people were gathering their camp chairs and bringing out coolers. Kids shoved hot dogs and marshmallows on sticks and hovered them over orange flames.

A group of hikers huddled around the warm glow of the campfire talking late into the night.

"Did you hear that?" Adam said nervously, looking back at the dark forest behind him.

"Hear what?" Theo laughed. "You're not scared, are you?"

"Yeah right," Adam sneered. "My mind must be playing tricks on me."

"Or not," Abraham, the oldest of the group said. "You do know that _____ Cave has got its very own ghost."

The men laughed and urged Abraham to continue on.

"Well," he said slowly. "No one knows when this story actually takes place. All we know is that it was published on ___/_____ by someone named _____ _____. It's about a girl named Melissa and her unrequited love: a tutor by the name of Mr. _____. The story goes that this girl Melissa was a wild child and was hard to contain until he came along."

"Ah come on, Abraham," one of the young men cried. "A love story?"

THE GHOST

"Oh but this one is different. A Southern girl like her falling for a _____. It was scandalous if anyone found out. She finally couldn't take it anymore and told him how she felt. After they spoke he didn't see her again.

He stayed around town though tutoring other students. A few months later, the town was all excited to hear that Mr. _____ was engaged.

Now Melissa's got a secret. Not too far from her house lies the _____ Cave. She knows the cave better than anyone else in town. One fateful night, Mr. _____'s wedding party is passing the cave. Melissa happens to be there and sees them. They all get on a ferry to cross the lake but there's too many people. They all can't fit.

Someone has to stay behind and it is none other than Mr. _____."

"Wait a minute," Casper asked, "the guy getting married stays behind?"

"Weird, I know," continued Abraham, "but that's how the story goes. Imagine poor Melissa minding her own business and there he is. She didn't know what to do. She was heartbroken but still excited to see him. She takes a chance and goes up to him.

It's all happening fast and before she could really think about what she was doing, she tells him there's a special passageway in the Cave that will get him to the other side before the ferry. He believes her! Mr. _____ follows her into the Cave but only Melissa comes out."

"So what happened?" Adam stuttered.

THE GHOST

"She lures him into the cave. She's still in love with him but she also wants a little revenge. Melissa's got the _____ and she is leading him through the cave. When they get far enough in she smashes the _____ and hides. She wants to hear him beg. She thought he would stay where he was but he goes deeper into the cave. Now she doesn't know what to do. His voice is trailing off but it's dark and she can't find him. Eventually he gets so far in that she can't hear him and she crawls back out."

"Did he make it out?" Casper asked.

"No," Abraham said with a shrug. "The townspeople searched the Cave for weeks looking for any sign of life. All they ever found was a _____."

"What about Melissa? Did they think she did it?" asked Theo.

Abraham's smile fell and he spoke in a hushed voice, "Melissa was quiet about the whole thing. No one ever knew she was there. Eventually the town moved on but she never did. Now she is old, sick and about to die. She never told anyone and the guilt is tearing her apart. She returns to the cave to punish herself by going through what he did. No one ever saw her again."

"So she died in the cave?" asked Adam.

"No one knows. But to this day people swear they hear a wailing voice in that part of the cave."

"You're lying," Casper said shakily.

Abraham leaned back in his chair with an arched

THE GHOST

brow, "I wish I was. This all happened a long time ago and they never found anything. Just wait. Tomorrow when we go in the cave maybe you'll hear it too."

This story was originally written under a pen name.

Use the story clues in the puzzles to answer the question below.

What is the author's real name?

_____

Write the clues from the puzzles in the spaces below. Complete the story by figuring out where the clues fit in the story.

Story Clues:

_____
_____
_____
_____
_____
_____
_____
_____

PUZZLE INSTRUCTIONS

Puzzle 24: Cryptogram

Solve the cryptogram to decode a phrase. Once you have decoded the phrase, answer the question at the bottom of the puzzle for the story clue.

Puzzle 25: Sudoku

Solve the puzzle by filling in each box, row, and column with the numbers 1 through 9. Remember that there cannot be two of the same number in a box, row, and column. Once you have finished the puzzle, drop the circled numbers down and you have your story clue.

Puzzle 26: Framework

Use the word bank to solve the puzzle. There are 7 circled letters in this puzzle. Once you have collected all the letters unscramble them to get your story clue.

Puzzle 27: Codebreaker

Each letter has a numerical value. You have been given two letters to start. Use the given letters and find their numbers in the puzzle to fill in the alphabet key. Once you have the alphabet key, use it to decode the story clue at the bottom of the puzzle.

Puzzle 28: Codebreaker

Same as Puzzle 27.

PUZZLE INSTRUCTIONS

Puzzle 29: Word Search

Use the word bank at the bottom of the page to find the words in the puzzle. There are 4 intersecting letters in this puzzle. Write down the intersecting letters and unscramble for a story clue.

Puzzle 30: Crossword

There are a series of Across and Down clues you need to solve. The clues will give you the word you need to put in the puzzle. There are 9 circled letters in the puzzle. Collect the letters and unscramble.

THE GHOST

47

Puzzle 24: Cryptogram ㊲

```
XYPE    EQNXYAWJ    EXUXA    PE

RJQTJ    DQW    FUJB    XYPJIE.

PX'E    HPI    DQW    YQWEA

WUGPJI    UJL    CUWIA,    DUJGB

YUXE.

BQN    GUJ    EPX    LQTJ    XQ    U

JPGA    FAUC    QD    HUWHAGNA,

DWPAL    GYPGRAJ,    UJL    GQWJ

HWAUL.    PX'E    XYA    YQFA    QD

GQNJXWB,    OUSS,    UJL    HCNAE

-    XQIAXYAW    RJQTJ    UE

HCNAIWUEE.
```

WHAT STATE IS THIS? _____

THE GHOST

Puzzle 25: Sudoku 132

		8	7	1	4	○	2	9
2	7	5	9	8		6		
1	9	4	6	2		7	8	3
6	4				1	2	7	○
5		2	4	6	7	9	3	
	3	○			○	4		
	○	3	8	5		1		7
4	1	6		7	9	8	5	2
8	5	7				3	9	6

0 ___ ___ ___ ___ ___ ___

THE GHOST

Puzzle 26: Framework

4 LETTERS	BROOCH	8 LETTERS	9 LETTERS
TORC	CHOKER	BRACELET	MEDALLION
		EARRINGS	
6 LETTERS	7 LETTERS	LAPEL PIN	
AMULET	HAIRPIN	NECKLACE	
ARMLET	PENDANT	CUFFLINK	
BANGLE	TIE CLIP		

THE GHOST

Puzzle 27: Codebreaker 18

THE GHOST

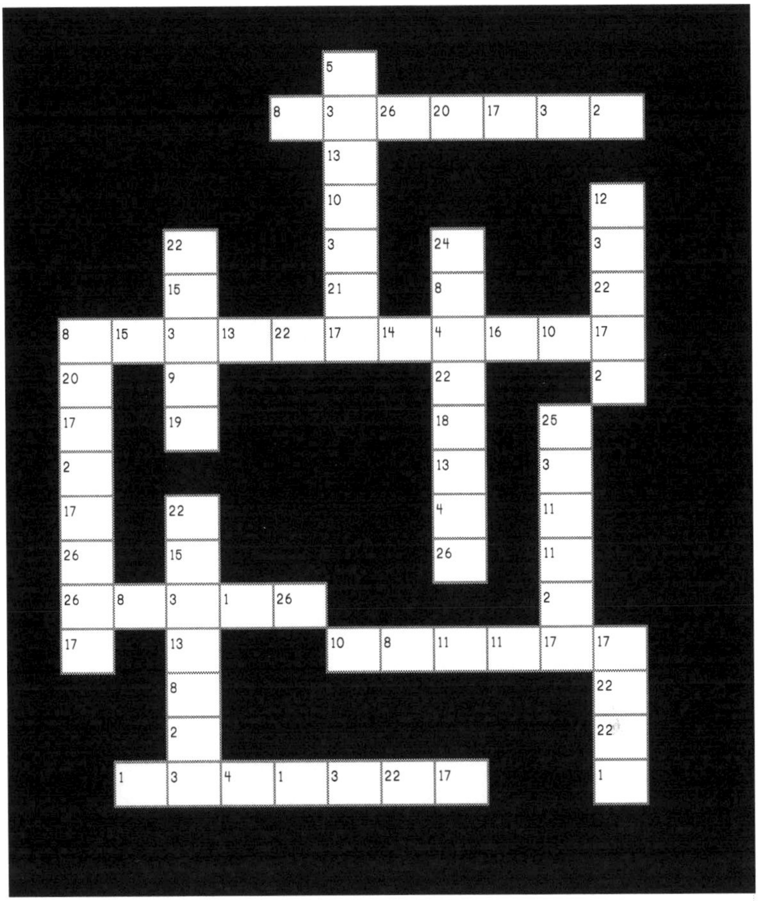

Puzzle 28: Codebreaker

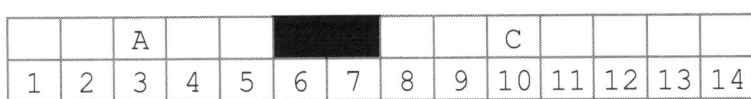

THE GHOST

Puzzle 29: Word Search

```
I L M H S M D E E K U L D N A H L O O C S Q L
V N W O D N I W R A E R T H E T H I R D M A N
C E E G C I T I Z E N K A N E W F J S Z O H L
F J R O C T P Y W P E E L S G I B E H T D Y A
R T C T I S A M C T O U C H O F E V I L E D W
A H W V I F J R F A L L A B O U T E V E R R R
N E T G B G T D U M S V A I L O E L D Y N A E
K G J N A N O D P A V A O A C C E B E R T V N
E R J O D W B S W A L C B J U T R Q M U I E C
N A H K L O V M E S T H E L E O P A R D M L E
S P S G A T M A R O M Y N J A X J U Q N E U O
T E U N N A K R W I V Y Y O W N V B E O S O F
E S R I D N E Y O S X A Y E I E C W J T O B A
I O D K S I S P J F K T R G Z S F A N T H T R
N F L R P H Y O Q R L A W B V M L O T A C E A
T W O Z X C Z P V I X E E C O C Y U U P Y S B
Q R G S I L O P O R T E M R E I B S P U S N I
Z A E M Z Y H I Z E O K K N F S R P F E P U A
W T H I K O P N X C I T Y L I G H T S P R S X
Y H T B H K A S E S I A R U M A S N E V E S G
```

ALL ABOUT EVE
BADLANDS
CASABLANCA
CHINATOWN
CITIZEN KANE
CITY LIGHTS
COOL HAND LUKE
FRANKENSTEIN
FREAKS
KING KONG
LAURA
LAWRENCE OF ARABIA
MARY POPPINS
METROPOLIS
MODERN TIMES
PATTON
PSYCHO
REAR WINDOW
REBECCA
REPULSION
RIO BRAVO
SEVEN SAMURAI
SUNSET BOULEVARD
THE BIG SLEEP
THE GOLD RUSH
THE GRAPES OF WRATH
THE LEOPARD
THE THIRD MAN
TOUCH OF EVIL
VERTIGO

THE GHOST

Puzzle 30: Crossword

ACROSS
1. LUNAR RAINBOW
2. SUNBEAMS, SUN RAYS, OR SPLINTERED LIGHT
3. A BRIGHT APPEARANCE OF THE SKY CAUSED BY REFLECTION FROM A DISTANT ICE SHEET
4. VERTICAL BEAM OF LIGHT
5. WHEN THE SUN SUDDENLY CHANGES OF COLOR FOR 1 OR 2 SECONDS
6. SNOW FORMATION AT HIGH ALTITUDES

DOWN
1. ELECTRICAL DISCHARGE CAUSED BY AN ERUPTION
2. NATURAL ELECTRICAL DISCHARGE BETWEEN A CLOUD AND THE GROUND
3. OBSCURED CLARITY BECAUSE OF DUST OR SMOKE
4. A ROTATING COLUMN OF WATER AND SPRAY FORMED BY A WHIRLWIND
5. REDDISH OR GREENISH LIGHT IN THE SKY, NEAR THE POLES
6. WALKING ROCKS

PUZZLE WORKSHEET

This is the end of the puzzles for The Ghost. Use this space to write down clues, unscramble words, take notes, and figure out how the missing words fit into the story.

THE STORYTELLER

My favorite time of day is early in the evening before dinner. Babies are napping while the older children play in the woods. The men and boys have left to catch fish and I get to spend quality time with the women in my family. It's just like every other day in the _____ tribe.

Usually we have time to relax and talk while we weave but we are too busy for that. My sister is getting married in a week and my family is anxiously preparing for her _____ ceremony. Every member of our tribe comes together to make lavish feasts and give gifts to the new couple.

I didn't know how to weave for the last ceremony but this time I can actually help. My grandmother is helping me make one of my first baskets. My favorite spot to weave is right next to her under the shade of tall _____ trees.

Even though she's older and her hands shake, she twists the _____ _____ in ways I cannot imagine. She is able to take several different colors of _____ and create pictures or special prayers on her baskets.

As the sun begins to lower and the earth cools, she tells me the stories that her grandmother used to tell her. She has a special way of making me feel like I am a part of the story.

One of my favorite stories is the one about the magical dance. A dance so beautiful everyone stops to watch. My grandmother has lived in _____ her whole life and has only seen it a couple of times.

No one knows when the magical dance will come but everyone eagerly waits. The dancers are graceful

THE STORYTELLER

and strong. They flicker and morph like the flames of a fire. They bob and sway like the ocean tide. They twirl and spin in a way that makes them look like they are flying through the trees.

Their movements bring playfulness and energy to the youth and remind the older ones that no one is ever truly gone. My grandmother said that if you look really close, you can see our ancestors among the dancers. They sing and sway and watch over us.

Someday I hope to learn that dance and be one of those who are fortunate enough to be among the _____.

What is the "magical dance" the grandmother speaks of?

_____

Write the clues from the puzzles in the spaces below.

Story Clues:

_____
_____
_____
_____
_____
_____
_____

PUZZLE INSTRUCTIONS

Puzzle 31: Codebreaker

Each letter has a numerical value. You have been given two letters to start. Use the given letters and find their numbers in the puzzle to fill in the alphabet key. Once you have the alphabet key, use it to decode the story clue at the bottom of the puzzle.

Puzzle 32: Crossword

There are a series of Across and Down clues you need to solve. The clues will give you the word you need to put in the puzzle. There are 6 circled letters in the puzzle. Collect the letters and unscramble.

Puzzle 33: Codebreaker

Same as 31.

Puzzle 34: Framework

Use the word bank to solve the puzzle. There are 5 circled letters in this puzzle. Once you have collected all the letters, unscramble them to get your story clue.

Puzzle 35: Word Maze

Your starting point is the circled letter. Use the words at the bottom of the page to find and mark them in the puzzle. Unlike word searches, the letters are not all in a straight line. These words can go up, down, forward, and backward.

As you solve the maze, the trail will double back on itself 6 times. Collect the 6 letters that intersect and unscramble them for the story clue.

PUZZLE INSTRUCTIONS

Puzzle 36: Codebreaker

Same as Puzzle 31.

Puzzle 37: Cryptogram

Solve the cryptogram to decode a phrase. Once you have decoded the phrase, answer the question at the bottom of the puzzle for the story clue.

Puzzle 38: Codebreaker

Same as Puzzle 31.

THE STORYTELLER

Puzzle 31: Codebreaker 72

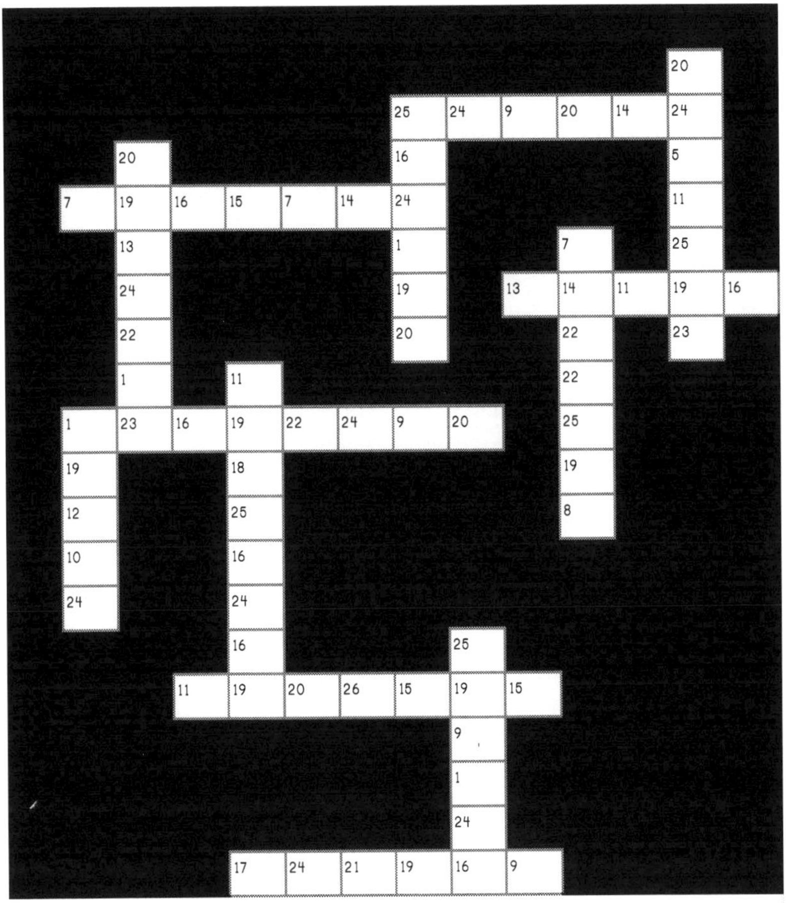

1	2	3	4	5	6	7	8	9	10	11	12	13	14

				O			L				
15	16	17	18	19	20	21	22	23	24	25	26

___ ___ ___ ___ ___ ___ ___ ___

15 5 9 15 14 10 1 22

THE STORYTELLER

Puzzle 32: Crossword

ACROSS
1. TO IMPROVISE AND DELIVER WITHOUT PREPARATION
2. CAMERA MOVES ALONGSIDE SUBJECT
3. SPOOL FOR MOVING PICURES
4. ABRUPT TRANSITION
5. PAIR OF BOARDS TO AID SOUND SYNCHRONIZATION
6. PLOT DEVICE OFTEN USED IN THRILLERS

DOWN
1. A SURVEY OR REVIEW OF A PAST COURSE OF EVENTS OR PERIOD OF TIME
2. CHIEF LIGHTING TECHNICIAN
3. A PERFUNCTORY PERFORMANCE OF A PLAY OR ACTING PART
4. LOW BUDGET FILM
5. OCCURRING, APPEARING, OR CHANGING AT USUALLY IRREGULAR INTERVALS : OCCASIONAL
6. NON-NARRATIVE VISUAL/SOUND EXPERIENCE WITH NO STORY AND NO ACTING

THE STORYTELLER

Puzzle 33: Codebreaker ②

THE STORYTELLER

Puzzle 34: Framework

3 LETTERS
IVY

5 LETTERS
HAKEA

6 LETTERS
DAPHNE
PRIVET

7 LETTERS
BRAMBLE
CALLUNA
JASMINE
VERVAIN

8 LETTERS
HIBISCUS
NINEBARK
OLEANDER

9 LETTERS
DOGHOBBLE

11 LETTERS
BOTTLEBRUSH
LINGONBERRY

THE STORYTELLER

Puzzle 35: Word Maze

```
V H C I C O N B V A E A C H S A N E B
E E X W R I E E U J B E D B H N T N E
N S N D Y S N A A K E W C H L P A L U
I S U N A S H C L U L S Y V O O C O H
C U D A Y I H C N O T Y A D Z U R J R
E Y B R H M A R A C R B J H E P B D Y
B B M T I D R O B M Y Y I D O C M E N
E W O E L O L D E H G W E N A E K Y O
A O E M M R L N A A U C M A S A L V L
C L W N I E Y O C M K K F L E N L I S
H U Q D Y I V K H E H O R S R C O N C
W H T O T P M A H K K S N I K I R A H
I T H B O L E L E Y E O S Y N T A B U
L E V O N B E I C T B N N E E Y C E M
D C I H A E T T C I A S O (C) J H C A T
W D R E C H S N A L T Y E E Y S H O G
O O G W D B U D L R O W N S I D E R O
G R I N I A B E A C H J E R N E Y C S
```

1. CONEY ISLAND
2. OCEAN CITY
3. CAROLINA BEACH
4. JENKINSONS
5. ATLANTIC CITY
6. KEMAH
7. MYRTLE BEACH
8. SANTA CRUZ
9. DAYTONA BEACH
10. HAMPTON BEACH
11. STEEL PIER
12. OLD ORCHARD
13. MISSION BEACH
14. SANDWICH
15. VENICE BEACH
16. WILDWOOD
17. REHOBOTH
18. VIRGINIA BEACH
19. JERSEY SHORE
20. DISNEY WORLD

64

THE STORYTELLER

Puzzle 36: Codebreaker 16

THE STORYTELLER

Puzzle 37: Cryptogram (30)

```
A C    D V    J A C    T C V J    I F D C Z Y    O

G O Z    R X E W Y    C S C F    A O S C .

A C    D V    V G O F J    O Z Y    T F O S C .

A C    D V    W X S D Z L    O Z Y    N D Z Y .

A C    L X C V    M A C F C S C F    P X E    L X .

J A D V    V X E Z Y    J A O J    A C    G O N C V

R O Z    M O F Z    X I    Y O Z L C F    X F

V A X M    P X E    A X M    A O K K P    A C    D V .

D J    D V    W X E Y    O Z Y    V A O F K .
```

WHAT IS THIS SOUND CALLED? _____

THE STORYTELLER

Puzzle 38: Codebreaker 102

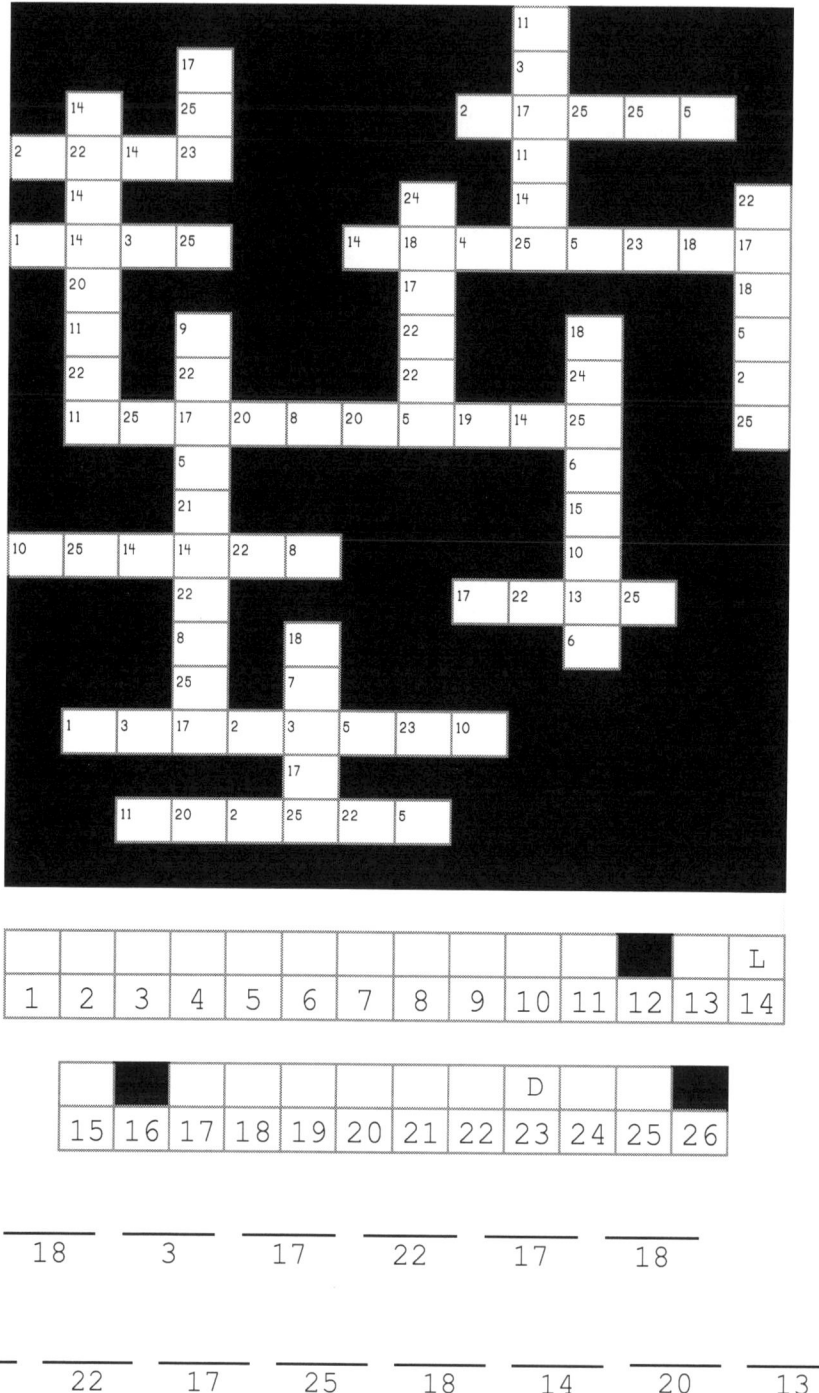

PUZZLE WORKSHEET

This is the end of the puzzles for The Storyteller. Use this space to write down clues, unscramble words, take notes, and figure out how the missing words fit into the story.

THE BARGAIN

"Where am I going?" a man uttered as he staggered forward, his question echoing on the walls.

For hours he had been walking a dark, lonely path in the _____ and now there was light. The room was completely empty save for one passageway at the back of the hall. If a _____ light wasn't spilling out of the room, he wouldn't have known it was there.

He cautiously walked toward the light, afraid of what he would find. Shadows flickered across the floor and he stopped, hesitating to move forward. After one final look at the empty hall he walked into the light, following the stone steps.

As he drew closer, he began to hear voices.

"Ah, this boy has a strong _____," a low, weathered voice croaked.

"Of course he does," a woman remarked. "Look who his father is."

"Well he's gonna need all the strength he can get!" another voice cackled.

"Silence!" the weathered voice cried.

The man immediately backed himself against the wall, trying to control his heavy breaths.

"We have a visitor," the voice continued.

The man moved to run but was stopped by a woman. He shouted in surprise and leapt back. Staring straight at him was a younger woman with long dark hair and bright _____ eyes.

THE BARGAIN

"Now where did you come from?" she said with a small smile.

Before the man could say anything, she slung her arm around him and directed him into the room. In the center of the room was a platform with three stools, a large _____, and one long _____. Two women were seated there watching him closely with their _____ eyes as their companion walked him in.

The oldest woman, with long gray hair rose to her feet and shouted, "How many times have I told you not to bring in a wandering _____?"

The young woman opened her mouth to speak but the third woman interrupted, "I don't believe he is wandering."

The old lady sat back on her stool.

The young woman's smile fell as she withdrew from the man looking directly in his eyes, "I remember you. You were reckless."

"That's fitting for a child of _____," the old lady said with a grin.

The third woman placed her hand on the _____, averting her gaze from the young man, "I suppose your father sent you."

"What if he did?" the young man asked nervously.

"I'm not surprised," the third woman replied. "_____ loves a good bargain. Tell me... what is it that he wants this time?"

THE BARGAIN

The young man cleared his throat, shifting nervously on his feet. He could feel the three sets of _____ eyes peering into his soul. They already knew what he was asking for but they wanted to hear him say it.

He might be a hero but nothing was nearly as frightening as these women. They were unpredictable and held too much power. But that was something he would never say aloud.

Drawing in a deep breath the man shifted his gaze to each of the women and spoke. "_____ requests a trade. My life for another."

"Why would we do that?" the third woman questioned.

"Because you know my work isn't finished."

Silence fell over the room as the three women contemplated his response. The man immediately doubted his actions.

Who was he to question them? To suggest that something they had done was wrong? If they were offended, they might as well condemn him on the spot despite his father's status.

"Go on," the third woman said to the man's surprise.

"I have to go back. With every day that passes, my brother is wreaking havoc on humans. Innocent humans who know nothing of our world. I'm the only person who can stop him. I've gotten godly approval now all I need is you."

THE BARGAIN

The young man kept his gaze on the third woman. He wasn't entirely sure why but for some reason, he knew that she was the one he had to convince.

He drew in a slow breath and shrugged his shoulders, "I know this isn't typical but you know that I'm right. I can tell."

The third woman's expression shifted into a grin, "I've been waiting a long time for this. You have a deal, hero."

Name the three women.

_____, _____, _____

Write the clues from the puzzles in the spaces below. Complete the story by figuring out where the clues fit in the story.

Story Clues:

_____
_____
_____
_____
_____
_____
_____
_____

Puzzle 39: Codebreaker

Each letter has a numerical value. You have been given two letters to start. Use the given letters and find their numbers in the puzzle to fill in the alphabet key. Once you have the alphabet key, use it to decode the story clue at the bottom of the puzzle.

Puzzle 40: Codebreaker

Same as Puzzle 39.

Puzzle 41: Word Search

Use the word bank at the bottom of the page to find the words in the puzzle. There are 7 intersecting letters in this puzzle. Write down the intersecting letters and unscramble for a story clue.

Puzzle 42: Word Search

Use the word bank at the bottom of the page to find the words in the puzzle. There are 5 intersecting letters in this puzzle. Write down the intersecting letters and unscramble for a story clue.

Puzzle 43: Framework

Use the word bank to solve the puzzle. There are 6 circled letters in this puzzle. Once you have collected all the letters, unscramble them to get your story clue.

Puzzle 44: Crossword

There are a series of Across and Down clues you need to solve. The clues will give you the word you need to put in the puzzle. There are 6 circled

PUZZLE INSTRUCTIONS

letters in the puzzle. Collect the letters and unscramble.

Puzzle 45: Cryptogram

Solve the cryptogram to decode a phrase. Once you have decoded the phrase, answer the question at the bottom of the puzzle for the story clue.

Puzzle 46: Codebreaker

Same as Puzzle 39.

THE BARGAIN

Puzzle 39: Codebreaker 55

THE BARGAIN

Puzzle 40: Codebreaker 27

THE BARGAIN

Puzzle 41: Word Search ④

```
M N O T T O C E P F R S Z P E Y E S R E J O I
Q H E E I B G C C G F B V J A C X Z X L X C C
F T K X Y X I L B E A K S E A R Y E H E X R H
D O Z C L J S H Q Q E E U L D U T Q N L N T I
U C A F O Z X D V S F L J H W A I U L A U M F
L I W C K R Z M P L F R F U L X F M E S H A F
W R S P A N D E X P O W D O Q B V S I T Q X O
P T H M B D P U X F E C Z B R U Y I W A I E N
I G A I V H H X R F S G K P X C I S P N D L C
R E T S E Y L O P O D I Q B M F I A X E U Y W
N V N Y L O N I P Q Y V Y Y Y L P M R Y Y C Y
D A E H W V A M B E M A L C K H O Y J E S R I
Y B N K C I L W O O L E E P D E W D R N Y A I
X M I V P S F P E V M T E V L E V E R E N O V
R T L H P G O P O L Y C O T T O N T V Y T Q S
F I B V N H E S J I N O Y A R W N E R E I C A
M N O N V R M B E L R T Z O K K R U O L E V T
D K M J C L D D S A V N A C B R L X X E D S I
W Q M C X J A C Q U A R D K D X C W O T N M N
C E T A T E C A O V W Z R E B I F O R C I M S
```

ACETATE	KNIT	POLYCOTTON
CANVAS	LACE	POLYESTER
CHIFFON	LAMÉ	RAYON
CORDUROY	LATEX	SATIN
COTTON	LINEN	SILK
CRÊPE	LYCRA	SPANDEX
ELASTANE	MESH	TRICOT
EYELET	MICROFIBER	VELOUR
JACQUARD	MICROFLEECE	VELVET
JERSEY	NYLON	WOOL

THE BARGAIN

Puzzle 42: Word Search

```
X P N D F O H T U B L O W G U N W P P S P M X
L I S K J A V E L I N C G U H S E Z P Z R V B
D H Q R S W A H O G E D A N E R G E V D M A O
J W Y J O O T C J C B O P S M M A X Q A T B O
D L N Y H H L T Z Q W C E I M R P X U O C D M
S L L M P Q A A Z S T T Z E H L A I M S L F E
H U Q E I F T H Y L Y D D U I V M A J D A U R
I B U T X U L O C I M R E M M A H R A W Y Q A
L H A R P O O N V A H P E Y Z A M Y E L M N N
L R R I Z R J J O L G A R Y W X X Z I J O O G
E A T L P U T W W F V H S K V H S L V R R N S
L T E Z E Y D E O P W V E M V G S I B X E N B
A S R I V T S Z K B Z F B R M U N O C N A A W
G G S M I M T F L S N M N F I O K I I K O C O
H N T O A L Y T C O U M T S L O Z L L T L W B
K I A U L N O Y U R W M X W V F L J P S M E G
T N F W G E T G B T Q Q L A Q E U O V E Z G N
H R F K D H L Z U A L O N G S W O R D Z C R O
U O B B E I P G L G K C A N A T A K O X S A L
D M Q M G I O H C C R O S S B O W S N S A V M
```

ATLATL
BLOWGUN
BOOMERANG
BULLWHIP
CANNON
CLAYMORE
CLUB
CROSSBOW
DOLOIRE
FLAIL

GLAIVE
GRENADE
HARPOON
HATCHET
JAVELIN
KATANA
LONGBOW
LONGSWORD
MACE
MORNING STAR

MUSKET
QUARTERSTAFF
SCYTHE
SHILLELAGH
SICKLE
SLING
SPEAR
TOMAHAWK
WARHAMMER
XIPHOS

THE BARGAIN

Puzzle 43: Framework

5 LETTERS	6 LETTERS	7 LETTERS	8 LETTERS
COBRA	FRENCH	CROCHET	FISHTAIL
CROWN	SPIRAL	FEATHER	MILKMAID
DUTCH	ZIG ZAG	GODDESS	
GREEK	ZIPPER	LATTICE	9 LETTERS
TWIST		MERMAID	WATERFALL
		REVERSE	

THE BARGAIN

Puzzle 44: Crossword

ACROSS
1. KNOWN TO BE TRUE
2. MUTUAL RELATIONSHIP BETWEEN TWO THINGS
3. QUOTE SOMETHING AS EVIDENCE FOR AN ARGUMENT OR STATEMENT
4. TRUSTED ADVISOR
5. SOMETHING THAT DEVIATES FROM WHAT IS STANDARD OR EXPECTED

DOWN
1. ROOM EQUIPPED FOR EXPERIMENTS
2. PROCEDURE TO MAKE A SCIENTIFIC DISCOVERY
3. UNCHANGING STANDARD FOR A SURVEY
4. ASSEMBLED SPECTATORS
5. PROOF
6. DIAGRAM SHOWING RELATION BETWEEN VARIABLES
7. PHYSICAL EQUILIBRIUM

THE BARGAIN

Puzzle 45: Cryptogram 154

```
DJ'V    JDGC    JX    YOZRC!
JAC    WDLAJⓋ    OFC    WXM.    JAC
GEVDR    DV    WXEY.

JOK    PXEF    JXC    JX    ⒿAC
TCOJ    OZY    LCJ    XEJ    XI
PXEF    VCOJ.
MOJRA    JAC    YⒹVRX    TOWW

VⓀDZ    OFXEZY    OZY    IXWWXM
JAC    RFXMY.
QEGK    OZY    VAXEJ.
JMDVJ    OZY    JEⒻZ.

WCJ'V    YOZRC    JAC    ZⒹLAJ
OMOP!
```

___ ___ ___ ___ ___ ___ ___

THE BARGAIN

Puzzle 46: Codebreaker

PUZZLE WORKSHEET

This is the end of the puzzles for The Bargain. Use this space to write down clues, unscramble words, take notes, and figure out how the missing words fit into the story.

TRUE FORM

The house was quiet. The bed was empty. His beloved ship was in pieces. All that was left of their loving husband and father was a memory. With nothing but a small trunk and some food, the woman and child set out in search of a new home.

"Mother, is this it?" Isla asked as they approached a large cave.

Nerissa smiled at the familiar sight and gripped her daughter's hand, "Yes! I used to go here all the time with my friends. This was like my second home."

Nerissa shifted the trunk in her arms as she spoke, "Ever since you were a little baby I've wanted to take you here but I couldn't. I knew that once I came back I would never want to leave. It looks just like it did when I left."

"It's pretty," Isla said as she looked over the beautiful _____. "How are your friends going to meet you here?"

"Come sit with me," Nerissa said as she sat down on the ground. "There's something I need to tell you before we go in."

"This is where I met your father," Nerissa started.

"Really?" Isla exclaimed.

"Really," Nerissa said with a nod. "Just a couple miles away from this cave is where our family started. This place is very important to me. It taught me who I was and I figured it was time I do the same for you."

TRUE FORM

Nerissa pulled a gold chain off her neck taking one last look at the rusty key. She turned the trunk toward her and slid the key into the keyhole.

With a small click, the trunk opened and inside lie two ____ _____. They were cold and wet with one significantly smaller than the other.

Nerissa shook her head slowly at the sight as she carefully pulled them out. Before she could get out a single word, Isla grabbed the smaller one from her mother, looking at it with wide eyes.

"Where did you get this?" Isla gasped.

"It's yours."

"I knew it!"

"You knew..." Nerissa said in surprise.

"Dad told me that we were different," Isla said with a smile. "He said that there was a reason we were always drawn to the _____ but he wouldn't tell me what it was. He said that this would explain everything."

"It does." Nerissa said with a smile. "I know it may seem a little strange but you and I were born to be in the _____."

Isla shook her head in disbelief, "Other kids would say that they loved being in the _____ but I always knew it was different. It felt like I couldn't survive. I needed it."

Nerissa nodded slowly, watching the wheels turn in her daughter's head.

TRUE FORM

Isla looked down at her hands speaking softly, "This is why I have _____ _____. It's because I'm an... _____."

"Yes!" Nerissa exclaimed.

"But how are we human?"

"You are a _____ _____. You can switch between your true form and this one by putting on this _____. I hid our _____ so we would never be tempted to leave your father."

Tears brimmed in Isla's eyes, "And he knew why?"

"Yes. You see, humans don't live as long as we do," Nerissa said with a somber look. "I didn't expect your father to go so soon but we vowed that we would give you a chance to live both lives. Then once you were all grown up, you could choose for yourself."

Isla shook her head slowly, "So there are more like us?"

"A lot more!" Nerissa cried as she threw her arms in the air. "They've been waiting to meet you for years. I know it's a lot to take in but this is what your father wanted."

Isla nodded slowly, "I know. I just... I miss him so much."

Nerissa reached over and hugged her daughter tightly, "I miss him too. We will always have the memories of our time together. But now it's time I show you who you really are."

TRUE FORM

There is a specific name for this type of mythological creature.

What are Nerissa and her daughter?

_____

Write the clues from the puzzles in the spaces below. Complete the story by figuring out where the clues fit in the story.

Story Clues:

_____
_____
_____
_____
_____
_____
_____

PUZZLE INSTRUCTIONS

Puzzle 47: Word Search

Use the word bank at the bottom of the page to find the words in the puzzle. There are 6 intersecting letters in this puzzle. Write down the intersecting letters and unscramble for a story clue.

Puzzle 48: Cryptogram

Solve the cryptogram to decode a phrase. Once you have decoded the phrase, answer the question at the bottom of the puzzle for the story clue.

Puzzle 49: Word Maze

Your starting point is the circled letter. Use the words at the bottom of the page to find and mark them in the puzzle. Unlike word searches, the letters are not all in a straight line. These words can go up, down, forward, and backward.

As you solve the maze, the trail will double back on itself 5 times. Collect the 5 letters that intersect and unscramble them for the story clue.

Puzzle 50: Framework

Use the word bank to solve the puzzle. There are 5 circled letters in this puzzle. Once you have collected all the letters, unscramble them to get your story clue.

Puzzle 51: Codebreaker

Each letter has a numerical value. You have been given two letters to start. Use the given letters and find their numbers in the puzzle to fill in the alphabet key. Once you have the alphabet key, use it to decode the story clue at the bottom of the puzzle.

PUZZLE INSTRUCTIONS

Puzzle 52: Word Search

Use the word bank at the bottom of the page to find the words in the puzzle. There are 12 intersecting letters in this puzzle. Write down the intersecting letters and unscramble for a story clue.

Puzzle 53: Crossword

There are a series of Across and Down clues you need to solve. The clues will give you the word you need to put in the puzzle. There are 4 circled letters in the puzzle. Collect the letters and unscramble.

TRUE FORM

Puzzle 47: Word Search 34

```
E G A T T O C K A T R E T S N E U M U T T N T
G C C E K Z G C O L B Y J A C K M B A G X L S
J U H X C C P B U X O C Q Q L L I B O G I A T
Q N E E I C A E X I I Z E U L B U S O S W T I
K A U H D R M J P B A G N H B C M A D E T W L
Q S A O N D W R Y W W T W O W O T L C L R L T
W E C P N Y A G E E L Z E J G F H J W I O M O
B M U R Y W O R R Z R M E F S R G M E M F H N
X R T X E E A D U O G E B Q Z S O U E B E F R
A A T M I A Z N G W M X T K E S N G M U U I G
B P T R E B M E M A C Q Q N E T G E U R Q J X
Q O P R O V O L O N E F O L O Y Y I C G O C B
O N T X S H G F G X X P B I G M M R P E R T T
G W G N U N K R P R R N T N S F J B F R P J R
E V F E I W U L U A Z R V S W T L R V D F X O
H S B R Q Y J E C I A A X R I C O T T A W L F
C Y T M E B J S F V P A B J S A N G Z Z V I U
N S I R X R A F A Y K Q M C S N A C I R E M A
A M E H G M V H U J K C A J R E P P E P S K E
M L I L M O Z Z A R E L L A U E L J M F X U B
```

AMERICAN	FETA	MOZZARELLA
BEAUFORT	GOAT	MUENSTER
BLUE	GORGONZOLA	PARMESAN
BRIE	GOUDA	PEPPER JACK
CAMEMBERT	GRUYERE	PROVOLONE
CHEDDAR	HAVARTI	RICOTTA
COLBY JACK	LIMBURGER	ROQUEFORT
COTTAGE	MANCHEGO	STILTON
CREAM	MASCARPONE	STRING
EDAM	MONTEREY JACK	SWISS

TRUE FORM

Puzzle 48: Cryptogram

```
P O K    J C K Z P D C K    U C H E    P O K

N X Z J I    X Z W H H M    O Z L

_____    _____    G O F J O

E Z I K L    F P    K Z L F K C    P H

L G F E    Z M V    J Z P J O    T C K Q .
```

What special trait makes it easier to swim?
_____ _____

TRUE FORM

Puzzle 49: Word Maze

```
T R E C N O C T N D R S E D O O W B N
P D K I O P C E U P U N B D G F Y E O
O R E O P A Z L L A B K E I E H L L O
L I R T E C U C E S B P J S S E K S B
K A N U B O L Y P L U C E C N U U Y O
A B O L E R E U L A J O V O U K F R C
M E L U D M O L L S D U Y B O G E N N
E L E J M T H L T N E N I A Y M N I E
Y L U S E K R T E R S T R Y S R U F M
T Y O S L S D S D G E L E Y W D F E A
E C H A R Y F E V A R C H D I U W F L
M F A R L C O W U S E I B E N G L N C
O K D I E E L K H U V R E H G E O R P
V O A K S R N F R I I J P A T L C E L
U W B E T H E W J G S D S D J O E D R
P Z M T O U D A I L N T E M P O S O D
L D A L N E U G C L O E K N D R O M J
F E W C P C T N B R C F O P F A R Y A
```

1. CONTEMPORARY
2. MODERN
3. FLAMENCO
4. BOLLYWOOD
5. DISCO
6. BOUNCE
7. COUNTRY
8. SWING
9. TAP
10. JIVE
11. RAVE
12. FOLK
13. WESTERN
14. SALSA
15. PUNK
16. BALLET
17. CONCERT
18. POLKA
19. BOLERO
20. CAPOERIA
21. BELLY
22. CHARLESTON
23. LAMBADA
24. HOUSE

TRUE FORM

Puzzle 50: Framework

4 LETTERS
FOIL
GOLD
IRON
LEAD
ZINC

5 LETTERS
ALLOY
BRASS
STEEL

6 LETTERS
BRONZE
CHROME

COPPER
NICKEL
PEWTER
SILVER
SOLDER

7 LETTERS
MERCURY
TARNISH

8 LETTERS
GUNMETAL
TITANIUM
TUNGSTEN

TRUE FORM

Puzzle 51: Codebreaker 71

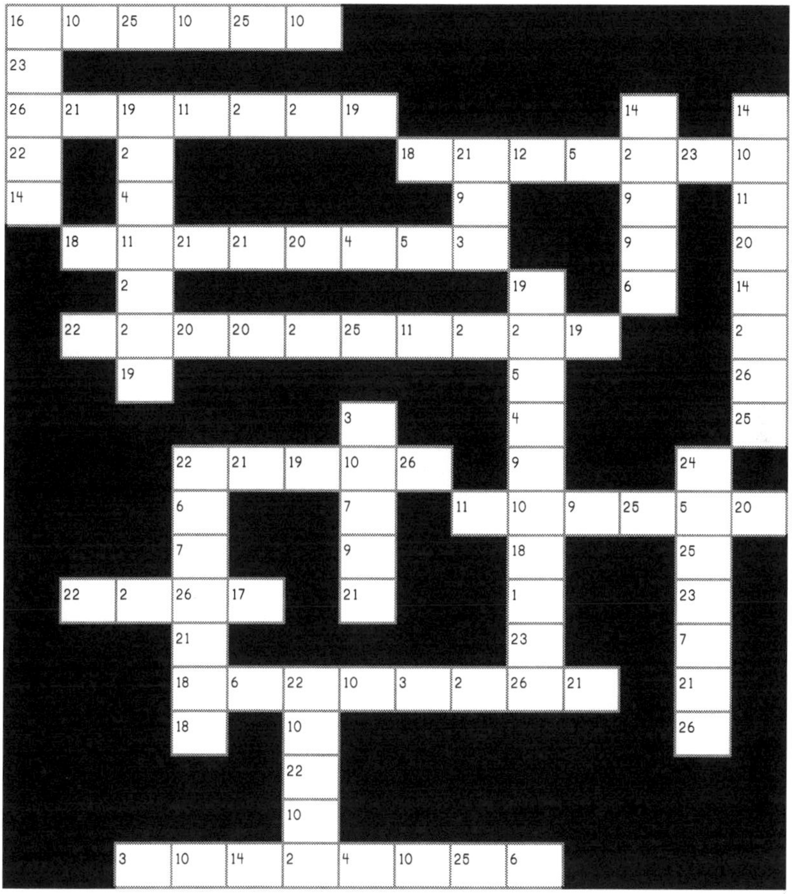

				U			■					■	
1	2	3	4	5	6	7	8	9	10	11	12	13	14

■							C				
15	16	17	18	19	20	21	22	23	24	25	26

___ ___ ___ ___ ___

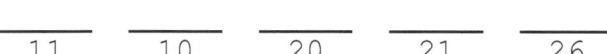

11 10 20 21 26

TRUE FORM

Puzzle 52: Word Search

```
J A S F T S U P M Y L O Y T W A V W R P Q B C
C N G I S B N R U B N A C N A C I L U V A G A
D N Q A X S O A A C O N C A G U A W O K U I U
C A L G R N P V V Y N O T E T D N A R G O O C
Q P Y K F R D O U E A L A T S A H S O B Y V A
S U E I K O H H Y G Q K V C L T U M J T Q L S
R R M N C H I M B O R A Z O N E W B F U J I U
Q N K A W R L N V S F O K N B A M C R Y S F S
Y A S B R E T F A O R A K I V D L D A C M I I
T X I A S T F E R Q A R J P T G D B D Z A S V
S I F L L T E P E T A C O P O P O E N K U S E
E Z B U D A T P N K R E J C S F C J U J N A N
R L W G N M I K E U I I L A N E D Z R U A M N
E L B A T W R V A W F V F B R R T C G S K N E
V F J U H X I K I L I M A N J A R O B U E O B
E B Y X P O C M K B T X S F L U I U B R A S M
R A S D A S H E N L Z I P H Y U K N N B Z N X
Y Q K U O X M Z F S R Z A C P P M R I L Q I U
D Y I S N R I T C E O D A M A V A N D E R V D
G I L M H W R A E W Y V S N N B S V D C R M R
```

ACONCAGUA
ALPS
ANNAPURNA
AORAKI
BEN NEVIS
BLANC
CAUCASUS
CHIMBORAZO
DAMAVAND
DENALI

ELBRUS
EVANS
EVEREST
FITZ ROY
FUJI
GRAND TETON
GRUNDARFJOROUR
KILIMANJARO
KINABALU
LICANCANBUR

MATTERHORN
MAUNA KEA
OLYMPUS
POPOCATEPETL
RAINIER
RAS DASHEN
SHASTA
TABLE
TIRICH MIR
VINSON MASSIF

Use the space on Page 93 to unscramble.

TRUE FORM

Puzzle 53: Crossword

ACROSS
2. EXTREME ANXIETY, PAIN OR SORROW
3. AREA ON CARRIER USED FOR TAKEOFF AND LANDING
4. ANY WIND THAT HAS A PERPENDICULAR COMPONENT TO THE LINE OR DIRECTION OF TRAVEL
5. TWISTING OF AN AIRCRAFT AROUND A VERTICAL AXIS
6. HEIGHT OF AN OBJECT IN RELATION TO SEA LEVEL OR GROUND LEVEL

DOWN
1. GOODS CARRIED
2. A STEP DOWNWARD IN A SCALE OF GRADATION
3. SMOOTH STRIP OF GROUND FOR LANDING
4. AUTHORIZATION FOR AN AIRCRAFT TO PROCEED ESPECIALLY WITH A SPECIFIED ACTION
5. FORCE THAT ACTS OPPOSITE OF THE MOTION
6. AIR TRAFFIC CONTROL _____
7. A FORCED LANDING WHEN AN AIRCRAFT LOSES ITS PROPULSIVE POWER

PUZZLE WORSHEET

96

Puzzle 52: Word Search Unscramble (159)

___ ___ ___ ___ ___

___ ___ ___ ___ ___ ___ ___ ___ ___

This is the end of the puzzles for True Form. Use this space to write down clues, unscramble words, take notes, and figure out how the missing words fit into the story.

POTS AND PANS

The boy ran.

His heart pounded fiercely against his chest as he raced through the streets. His feet ached. His lungs burned but he couldn't stop. He had promised his mother that if anything scary happened he would run home immediately.

So far the day had been normal. He'd gone to school in the morning just like every other day but then the noise started. His teacher tried to calm all the children but when she looked out, she told everyone to run home as fast as they could.

The boy did just that. He ran from the schoolhouse and into the marketplace. It was the only route that he knew to take. As he looked at the road ahead of him, fear filled his mind.

How could he get home through that?

All the buildings were empty and all the people were on the streets. Men were shouting. Women and children were screaming. Young men were ferociously banging on drums of all sizes with all the energy they had.

Every person old enough had pots and pans in their hands. There was banging and clashing and chanting everywhere he turned. His ears were ringing so badly he was afraid he'd lose his hearing.

One older woman was standing in the center of the street yelling at anyone who could hear her, "The _____ _____ have come! Lift up your voices! Grab everything you have! Make noise toward the _____!"

POTS AND PANS

Where the _____ used to be was a dark image moving across its surface, snuffing the light out slowly. The boy dodged and weaved through the crowded streets. He kept his eyes on the road ahead of him, counting how many times he turned.

It seemed impossible but somehow the noise was louder. The boy was moving as fast as he could, desperate to reach the safety of his mother's arms.

What was going on? Why is everyone acting like this?

Why were they all so loud?

As he ran he passed a small girl jumping up and down. Her hands were cupped around her mouth as she shouted, "Go away! Go away!"

The boy shoved his fingers in his ears in an effort to block out the sound. He was going to get through the crowd. He knew that if anyone could tell him what was going on, it was his mother. She always knew how to answer his questions.

"Go back where you came! Go back to _____ and return no more!" one elderly man cried.

"The _____ are here! The _____ are here!" Another woman wailed.

The boy turned one last corner and felt his heart leap at the sight of his mother.

To his surprise she too was banging pans together and shouting. His little sister was holding onto her leg and crying.

POTS AND PANS

His mother stopped and dropped the pans on the ground when she noticed her son. The boy made no effort to slow down as he crashed into his mother's arms.

"Everything will be alright, baby," his mother said as she kissed his head. "Everything will be okay."

He struggled to slow his breathing. Tears rolled down his cheeks as he squeezed his eyes shut. Maybe if he closed his eyes, it would all go away. He held an iron grip on his mother's leg refusing to let go.

"What's happening?" The boy asked with a quivering lip.

His mother gently pulled him away from her leg and gripped his hands tight, "Look at me."

The boy's eyes shifted to the fading _____ in fear.

His mother gripped his chin and forced him to look at her.

"Listen to me. Everything will be alright. I know it's scary but we must fight them," she said sternly. "They are called the _____. They have come to swallow the _____."

"Why? What are they?" the boy questioned.

"They are creatures sent from the _____ _____. Noise scares them. It is our job to make as much noise as we can to make them leave," his mother said, not looking away from him.

POTS AND PANS

She let go of his hands and motioned for the house, "Go. Grab our other pots! If we do it all together, it will work. Everything will be alright."

Where did people use noise to battle mythological creatures?

_____

Write the clues from the puzzles in the spaces below. Complete the story by figuring out where the clues fit in the story.

Story Clues:

_____
_____
_____
_____
_____
_____
_____

PUZZLE INSTRUCTIONS

Puzzle 54: Codebreaker

Each letter has a numerical value. You have been given two letters to start. Use the given letters and find their numbers in the puzzle to fill in the alphabet key. Once you have the alphabet key, use it to decode the story clue at the bottom of the puzzle.

Puzzle 55: Word Maze

Your starting point is the circled letter. Use the words at the bottom of the page to find and mark them in the puzzle. Unlike word searches, the letters are not all in a straight line. These words can go up, down, forward, and backward.

As you solve the maze, the trail will double back on itself 3 times. Collect the 3 letters that intersect and unscramble them for the story clue.

Puzzle 56: Framework

Use the word bank to solve the puzzle. There are 7 circled letters in this puzzle. Once you have collected all the letters, unscramble them to get your story clue.

Puzzle 57: Codebreaker

Same as Puzzle 54.

Puzzle 58: Crossword

There are a series of Across and Down clues you need to solve. The clues will give you the word you need to put in the puzzle. There are 6 circled letters in the puzzle. Collect the letters and unscramble.

PUZZLE INSTRUCTIONS

Puzzle 59: Word Search

Use the word bank at the bottom of the page to find the words in the puzzle. There are 9 intersecting letters in this puzzle. Write down the intersecting letters and unscramble for a story clue.

POTS AND PANS

103

Puzzle 54: Codebreaker 64

POTS AND PANS

Puzzle 55: Word Maze

```
E  S  P  O  L  V  H  F  E  I  M  I  A  P  R  I  C  O  T
D  Q  T  H  Y  R  R  E  B  E  S  W  O  F  Z  R  O  P  P
R  E  H  C  S  E  P  L  H  U  E  I  L  U  N  O  C  E  O
R  V  D  T  T  S  A  L  R  L  O (K) E  T  E  E  O  I  M
Y  E  O  E  R  W  R  R  D  B  O  B  F  G  D  E  C  V  E
B  T  O  S  A  L  G  O  O  T  P  E  U  R  T  Y  E  C  G
L  I  U  E  W  O  E  M  L  I  B  H  J  A  I  H  T  F  R
A  N  K  G  B  M  L  P  R  U  L  S  R  P  M  I  A  N  A
C  T  M  A  E  Y  A  P  D  R  K  D  W  E  F  R  K  N  F
K  L  S  V  R  R  V  U  N  F  U  O  N  B  R  U  I  T  I
B  O  E  A  D  D  E  S  U  K  C  A  J  E  G  P  T  H  L
E  G  G  R  E  U  T  W  C  D  G  P  O  X  N  E  N  O  O
R  H  U  O  N  E  U  E  A  T  N  A  C  E  A  Y  E  P  N
R  E  E  H  I  R  G  O  L  E  E  L  E  T  R  D  M  O  M
Y  Y  B  R  T  N  D  N  O  H  C  I  F  A  O  E  E  A  E
B  A  N  A  N  A  R  H  U  B  A  R  B  D  A  W  L  M  P
Y  U  D  R  E  I  D  F  P  N  I  O  F  W  V  G  C  A  F
H  D  E  O  M  E  L  C  E  S  W  J  T  Y  A  U  A  V  A
```

1. KIWI
2. APRICOT
3. POMEGRANATE
4. COCONUT
5. GRAPEFRUIT
6. HONEYDEW
7. GUAVA
8. ORANGE
9. JACKFRUIT
10. BLUEBERRY
11. STRAWBERRY
12. APPLE
13. GRAPES
14. CHERRY
15. BLACKBERRY
16. BANANA
17. RHUBARB
18. DATE
19. CANTALOUPE
20. CLEMENTINE

___ ___ ___

POTS AND PANS

Puzzle 56: Framework 151

4 LETTERS
GOLF
POLO
POOL

5 LETTERS
CHESS
RUGBY

6 LETTERS
HOCKEY
RACING
SKIING
SOCCER
TENNIS

7 LETTERS
AIRSOFT
ARCHERY
CYCLING

8 LETTERS
AQUABIKE
FOOTBALL
HANDBALL

10 LETTERS
BASKETBALL
VOLLEYBALL

POTS AND PANS

Puzzle 57: Codebreaker 106

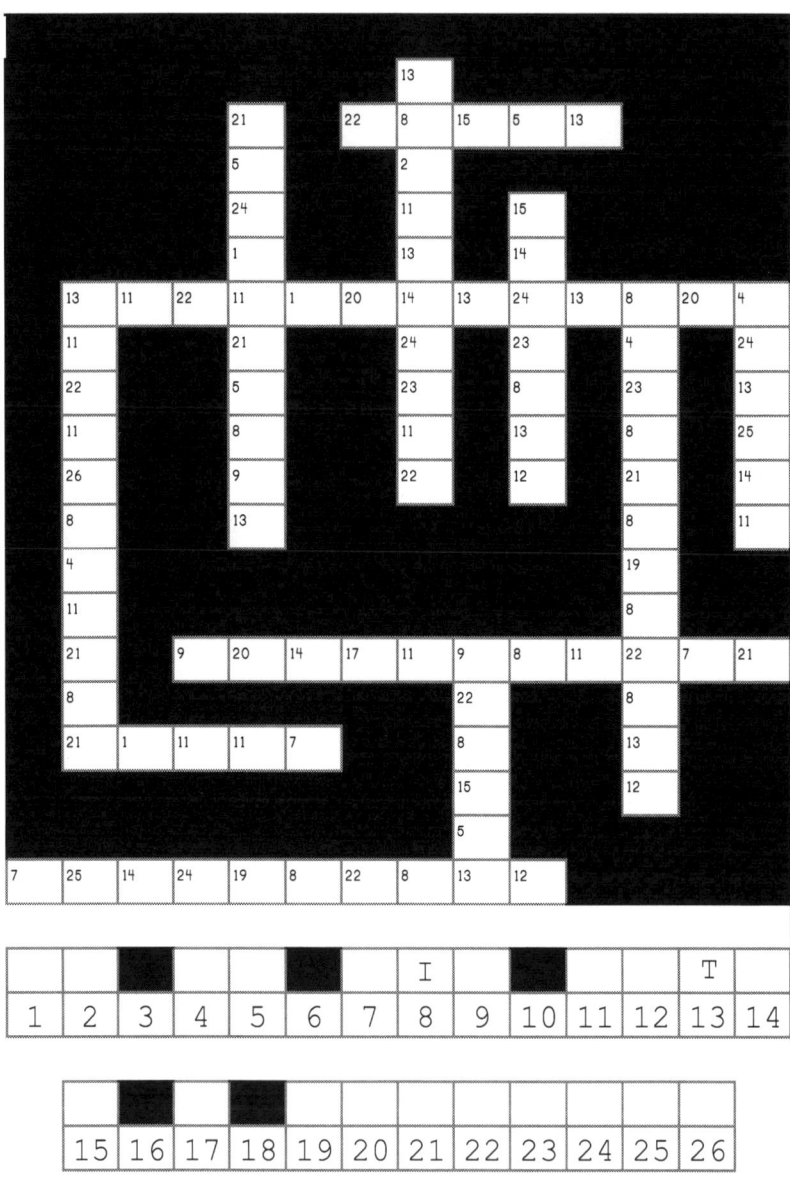

POTS AND PANS

Puzzle 58: Crossword

ACROSS
1. FIRM IN SPITE OF OPPOSITION
2. CAPACITY TO ENDURE PAIN
3. SHOWING A FONDNESS OF CAUSING TROUBLE
4. ADVENTUROUS
5. CREDULOUS
6. INTENDING TO DO HARM
7. MODEST
8. CUNNING OR DECEITFUL

DOWN
1. TRIVIAL
2. LEADER AROUSING LOYALTY
3. DESIRE TO SUCCEED
4. CAREFUL NOT TO HURT OTHERS
5. READINESS TO GIVE MORE OF SOMETHING
6. SEEING THE WORST ASPECT OF THINGS
7. ACADEMIC OR BOOKISH

POTS AND PANS

Puzzle 59: Word Search

```
S V T X S G D E E I P M A E R C T U N O C O C
R F B O R Z Z K C H E E S E C A K E A L C A U
P A R F A I T A P I I E I P E M I L Y E K T B
N O A A Q P K C E E H P O U N D C A K E I M E
B R O W N I E T K G A H N S N X O T H L N E Z
K W T H E P G E A U Z D O T E Z A N H P G A X
S B W O K A X V C L A W N E A P H Q U Q C L E
O S E O A N D L T F Q O I U Z E M T B T A C I
O O K P C O X E R L H P W R S Q Q W S X K O P
R P A I L C L V I O E E E M J M A T S S E O N
E A C E E H R D D M K S I T A C A F M Q N K I
H I T P N A J E E U V G E P U I F E O L U I K
C P O I N Z Q R C Q K K X A E U S S R V F E P
T I R E U R C L E L A F W V O L S O E C O N M
O L R R F N L I T C J E P K Z C P B R D E X U
C L A M O B D N P R V F U G Q I L P G B G C P
S A C T Z N E U V Y V F U J V L W O A K M F I
R D S X O W C W K E K A C D O O F L E G N A K
F O B L U E B E R R Y P I E G E I P N A C E P
B S B T N R O C L E M A R A C E T E K P M D V
```

AMBROSIA
ANGEL FOOD CAKE
APPLE PIE
BLONDIE
BLUEBERRY PIE
BOSTON CREME PIE
BROWNIE
CARAMEL CORN
CARROT CAKE
CHEESECAKE
COCONUT CREAM PIE
CUPCAKE
DIRT CAKE
DONUT
FUDGE
FUNNEL CAKE
ICE CREAM SUNDAE
KEY LIME PIE
KING CAKE
OATMEAL COOKIE
PANOCHA
PARFAIT
PECAN PIE
POUND CAKE
PUMPKIN PIE
RED VELVET CAKE
S'MORE
SCOTCHEROOS
SOPAIPILLA
WHOOPIE PIE

PUZZLE WORKSHEET

This is the end of the puzzles for Pots and Pans. Use this space to write down clues, unscramble words, take notes, and figure out how the missing words fit into the story.

THE TRICKSTER

Deep in the forest was a plot of land that was completely empty. There were no trees or flowers, only grass. It wasn't very large but it was believed that the great god _____ would often appear there and speak to those who were worthy.

Legends told of the elaborate _____ _____ hid from the world but the trickster wanted them for his own. Most would say he was selfish because of it but he believed that he had a right to share those _____ with the world. Why should _____ be the only one who can benefit from them?

So the young trickster set out on a quest for knowledge.

He knew that the all-knowing and all-seeing god would never just hand over something so precious but he had a plan. He would have to prove his worth and pledge to do whatever the god asked him to. It was a price he was willing to pay for the treasure.

But the young trickster was frustrated. He had already completed three difficult tasks and had not yet received the gift. He didn't want to be rude but he had held up his end of the bargain.

"I have done what you asked!" _____ cried, staring up at the heavens. "What more do you want?"

The clouds around him began to darken summoning a low rumble but he wasn't frightened. He knew that this was how _____ communicated. He wouldn't dare show his true form to a simple being like him.

THE TRICKSTER

Angry and impatient, _____ threw his hands in the air and shouted, "I have tied the _____ to its branch! I have ensnared the _____ and tricked the _____! I…"

"I know what you have done," a loud yet calm voice spoke, startling _____.

Now that he knew _____ had arrived, he would have to be more careful with his responses. He had come this far to prove his worth and didn't want to throw it all away now.

"You have done well," _____ continued. "But you are not yet ready to receive the _____."

A flicker of fear ran down _____'s spine. Was that it? Had he failed? No, he couldn't have.

He waited patiently in the silence and contemplated begging for another chance but decided against it.

A few moments later, the voice continued, "You think you are clever. I want you to prove it. I have one final task for you. If you are able to complete it, I will give you the _____. If not, you will leave and never return."

_____ stayed silent. He knew he would be able to complete it but that still didn't stop the nerves. The thought of walking away with nothing made him sick to his stomach. If he failed, he would never be able to walk away and forget.

He would never forgive himself if he failed.

THE TRICKSTER

Mustering up his remaining courage, _____ replied firmly, "I will do anything you ask."

The clouds grew increasingly darker and seemed as if they were closing in on him. The rumble of thunder was louder now and he could see small streaks of lightning ready to release upon the earth.

Both _____'s mind and heart were racing with anticipation. Surely, he wouldn't kill him. Would he?

"Your final task is to bring me the invisible _____ and you will have your _____."

_____ opened his mouth to speak but was unable to get a single sound out. The _____? He couldn't be serious.

No one had ever caught her before.

_____ watched as the clouds began to swirl across the sky, drawing further away from the earth. Within a matter of moments, the clouds had disappeared and the bright hot sun was shining down on him.

He had heard about this _____ before. She was both feared and respected by every creature who knew her. Despite her ability to turn invisible at will, she was impatient and prone to anger.

If he could somehow find a way to keep her from disappearing and cloud her mind with rage, he was sure he would be able to bring her to _____.

THE TRICKSTER

113

He knew he would only have one shot but he was determined to accomplish it.

What is this trickster also known as?

_____

Write the clues from the puzzles in the spaces below. Complete the story by figuring out where the clues fit in the story.

Story Clues:

_____
_____
_____
_____
_____
_____
_____
_____

PUZZLE INSTRUCTIONS

Puzzle 60: Codebreaker

Each letter has a numerical value. You have been given two letters to start. Use the given letters and find their numbers in the puzzle to fill in the alphabet key. Once you have the alphabet key, use it to decode the story clue at the bottom of the puzzle.

Puzzle 61: Codebreaker

Same as Puzzle 60.

Puzzle 62: Framework

Use the word bank to solve the puzzle. There are 6 circled letters in this puzzle. Once you have collected all the letters, unscramble them to get your story clue.

Puzzle 63: Word Search

Use the word bank at the bottom of the page to find the words in the puzzle. There are 7 intersecting letters in this puzzle. Write down the intersecting letters and unscramble for a story clue.

Puzzle 64: Word Search

Use the word bank at the bottom of the page to find the words in the puzzle. There are 7 intersecting letters in this puzzle. Write down the intersecting letters and unscramble for a story clue.

PUZZLE INSTRUCTIONS

Puzzle 65: Word Maze

Your starting point is the circled letter. Use the words at the bottom of the page to find and mark them in the puzzle. Unlike word searches, the letters are not all in a straight line. These words can go up, down, forward, and backward.

As you solve the maze, the trail will double back on itself 5 times. Collect the 5 letters that intersect and unscramble them for the story clue.

Puzzle 66: Cryptogram

Solve the cryptogram to decode a phrase. Once you have decoded the phrase, answer the question at the bottom of the puzzle for the story clue.

THE TRICKSTER

Puzzle 60: Codebreaker (129)

THE TRICKSTER

Puzzle 61: Codebreaker 81

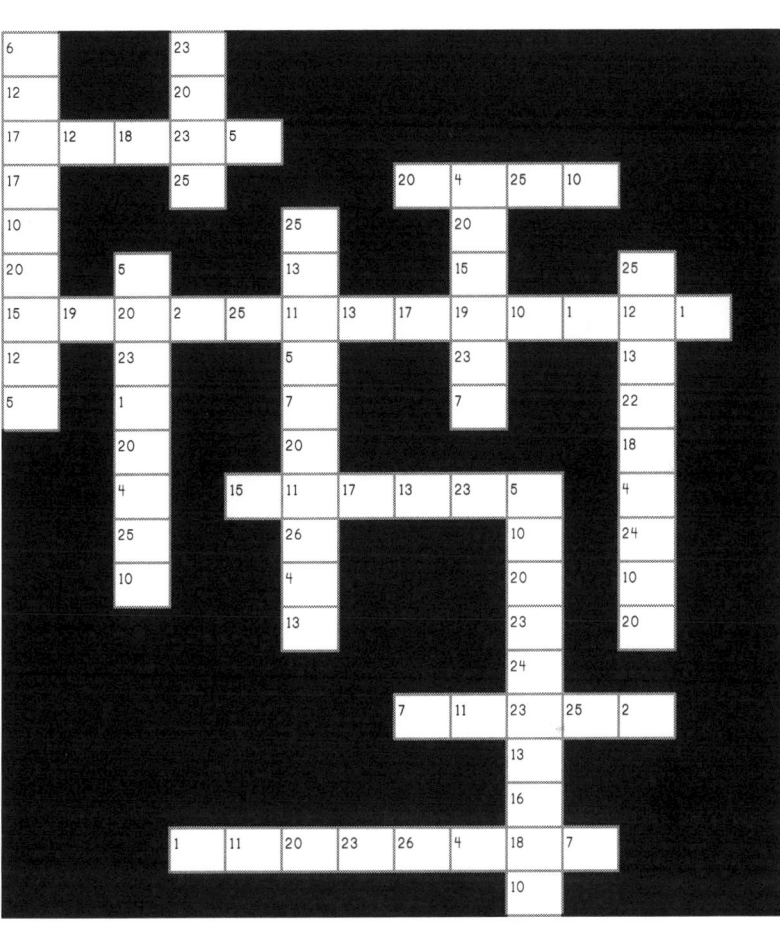

THE TRICKSTER

Puzzle 62: Framework

4 LETTERS
LION
SEAL

5 LETTERS
CLOWN
SNAKE
TIGER

7 LETTERS
TRAPEZE

8 LETTERS
ACROBATS
ELEPHANT
JUGGLING
UNICYCLE

9 LETTERS
KNIFE TOSS
STRONGMAN
TIGHTROPE

10 LETTERS
RINGMASTER
TRAMPOLINE

THE TRICKSTER

Puzzle 63: Word Search 89

```
B A S I T T E H G A P S F J I C U L L N Q L V
W G E N U V O L E Q N B E P Y H Q S H W K B P
R A D I A T O R I E Y L M X X K C E Y F I C G
E K A I L L I S U F L A Z Q L Z K C P G A H E
L M N T X B Y O W E F P J Z T G M N O R U G M
V X I F Z V T W T A Z O E V E Y C L R N G E I
V J D E T K Q A L J Y G L L C Z I M G C G N L
B E W J I Q I D D V T L G L L Z X E G B F V L
I I N E T L E M I L A S A G N A J U E Q E E I
Z E O I G B G D L N R Y C W G J F H C U T R C
Z B Y A D X A I E K I I W T X F V R B Z T M A
O E T L G L N V H T Z T T D R W S I A A U I P
G P H I X R A W E C P G A I M R D N X F C C E
N F L E N Q H F W T N E J C M G F A Z G I E L
I S I H N O U Y A J T O K T U O W Z W V N L L
R T B Y D N T F Q M F E C X Y B G Z C T E L I
T L I P C H E A E J M R B J E L L E T O R I N
S Z T V I C I P G I R E F F I H C M K I H N I
I V I P T T M Q T I D W W U S G H S T U U P A
A B Z J N M P P G I R O I F L I N G U I N E S
```

BAVETTE	GEMILLI	PICI
BIGOLI	GNOCCHI	RADIATORI
BUCATINI	GOMITI	RIGATONI
CAPELLINI	LASAGNA	ROTELLE
CHIFFERI	LINGUINE	SEDANI
CONCHIGLIE	MAFALDE	SPAGHETTI
FARFALLE	MAFALDINE	STRINGOZZI
FETTUCINE	MEZZANI	TAGLIATELLE
FIORI	NUVOLE	VERMICELLI
FUSILLI	PENNE	ZITI

THE TRICKSTER

Puzzle 64: Word Search

ANTARCTICA
ARABIAN
ARCTIC
ATACAMA
CHIHUAHUAN
COLORADO
DASHTE MARGO
GIBSON
GOBI
GREAT BASIN

GREAT SANDY
GREAT VICTORIA
KALAHARI
KARAKUM
KAVIR
KYZYLKUM
LIBYAN
LUT
MOJAVE
NAMIB

NEGEV
PATAGONIAN
REGISTAN
SAHARA
SIMPSON
SONORAN
SYRIAN
TAKLAMAKAN
THAR
YUMA

THE TRICKSTER

Puzzle 65: Word Maze

```
P R E Z E E W T H S U R B R U F G R F
L S E S E H S A L E S L V E N J O D E
O E Y E S H A D O W L A O D F M M W N
R B E N V J D S E N I F L W O P H S I
D E L S E U L B T F P E A D L D N T L
G N I A Y S U N N U G T T E D I L P O
S I N Z U H F O B Q L X W L K F I D G
P T E L R P I I U E O T D A U L A S M
R T R J I D E T M L S S E P M K N H U
A E S R M T D A B M B E Y W R C R C U
Y L B E E R P D R A R O W O E I E J R
O O E O P R E N O E T E P D A T M I L
E A L E R F O U N R E N J P H S D R E
C L T N I U N B Z C N C I L S P R P R
N A R I A M U P E R H I G H L I G E F
O W T M H E E N B U R C A R A L H C A
C X I E S C O N T O V S A M R E T R F
```

1. CONCEALER
2. FOUNDATION
3. BLUSH
4. PRIMER
5. PERFUME
6. HAIR TIES
7. CONTOUR
8. CREAM
9. BRONZER
10. HIGHLIGHTER
11. MASCARA
12. LIPSTICK
13. LASH CURLER
14. FACE PRIMER
15. NAIL POLISH
16. POWDER BRUSH
17. TWEEZERS
18. EYE SHADOW
19. LIP GLOSS
20. EYEBROW PENCIL
21. SHADOW PALETTE
22. FALSE LASHES
23. EYE LINER
24. SETTING SPRAY

___ ___ ___ ___ ___

THE TRICKSTER

Puzzle 66: Cryptogram

```
ZAOKO   VP   NIO   ZAVIQ   ZAFZ

ODOKT   HNJIZKT,   CONCYO,

FIB   YFIQJFQO   AFP   VI

HNRRNI.   ZAOPO   AFDO   SOOI

ZNYB   PVIHO   ZAO   SOQVIIVIQ

NU   ZVRO   FIB   CFPPOB   BNMI

ODOK   PVIHO.   MAFZ   FKO

ZAOT?
```

PUZZLE WORKSHEET

This is the end of the puzzles for The Trickster. Use this space to write down clues, unscramble words, take notes, and figure out how the missing words fit into the story.

THE GODDESS

"Go!" ____ cried as she pushed her younger siblings ahead of her.

If she had paid better attention she would have been able to get them to safety by now. She knew that her older sister would find them one day but she didn't expect it to be so soon.

_____ was ruthless when she was angry and _____ was afraid her wrath would kill them all.

The climb up _____ _____ was grueling but they had no choice. If they stopped, _____'s waves would crash over them and sweep them out to sea. _____ wasn't about to let that happen.

_____ focused all her energy on getting to the top passing her siblings quickly. Once she had swung over the edge, she stretched her arms out to pull everyone up. One by one, she pulled her siblings up despite the stabbing pain in her arms and shoulders.

As she pulled them, she told them to move to the edge furthest from the water. Clasping her last brother's wrists, she yelled as she pulled him over the edge.

Drenched in sweat and breathing heavily, _____ slumped against the edge, unable to move. She watched with blurry eyes as her siblings huddled together.

She could hear the crash of her sister's waves mix with her baby sister, ____'_____'s sobs.

_____ willed herself to her feet and hugged her siblings close, reassuring them.

THE GODDESS

They were all shaking with exhaustion and fear and many of them were crying. The sound alone filled _____ with rage.

How could she do this to them?

Was she always this cruel?

It had taken many long months of traveling to get away from her and to _____ and she wasn't about to give it up now.

She had the power to repel her sister and she was going to take back her paradise. No longer would they have to run from their sister's wrath.

"_____!" she shouted as she staggered toward the opposite edge, looking down at her sister's mighty waves.

She was frightened but her anger was stronger.

_____ threw her arms in the air and screamed, "Come and get me!"

The water roared in response and lunged for her.

The air thickened and grew hot. She could feel the warmth deep below the surface. It was slowly churning, eager to burst from it's prison. It sent a tingling feeling throughout her entire body.

Her hands shook with effort as she began to draw the fire out from below her feet. She gasped as the earth split beneath her.

Something orange bubbled under the surface just waiting for her to move it.

THE GODDESS

_____ watched as her sister tried in vain to reach her. She was too high. The fire was too strong.

_____ drew in a deep breath of the salty air.

This was it.

All her experimentation with fire had always been extinguished but now... there was no one to stop her.

With a cry of rage, _____ thrust her hands forward and a river of molten hot magma burst from the surface. It spewed over the edge and fell on the water.

The water sizzled under its intense heat and turned it into steam. _____ could hear her sister's cry of pain as the water began to retreat.

The lava flowed and _____ watched as the waves began to die down. She could see the form of her sister, injured and angry, swimming as far away from her as possible.

The ground around _____ began to cave in and formed a crater.

They were safe but __ was weak. Never before had she fought so hard. Her feet were burnt, her head was spinning, and her legs went limp.

_____'s mortal form died that day but her spirit lives on as the goddess of the volcanoes.

Special thanks to Tida from Kickstarter who provided the topic for this story. We loved learning about this one.

THE GODDESS

127

Her bones were buried deep in the hillside called _____ and the mountain remains alive to this day. Her fires stir within as both creator and destroyer. Some even say that if you look close enough at the fire, you can see her form looking back at you.

What is the name of this goddess' home?

_____

Write the clues from the puzzles in the spaces below. Complete the story by figuring out where the clues fit in the story.

Story Clues:

_____
_____
_____
_____
_____
_____
_____

PUZZLE INSTRUCTIONS

Puzzle 67: Codebreaker

Each letter has a numerical value. You have been given two letters to start. Use the given letters and find their numbers in the puzzle to fill in the alphabet key. Once you have the alphabet key, use it to decode the story clue at the bottom of the puzzle.

Puzzle 68: Cryptogram

Solve the cryptogram to decode a phrase. Once you have decoded the phrase, answer the question at the bottom of the puzzle for the story clue.

Puzzle 69: Codebreaker

Same as Puzzle 67.

Puzzle 70: Cryptogram

Same as Puzzle 68

Puzzle 71: Codebreaker

Same as Puzzle 67.

Puzzle 72: Codebreaker

Same as Puzzle 67.

THE GODDESS

Puzzle 67: Codebreaker 141

										C			
1	2	3	4	5	6	7	8	9	10	11	12	13	14

			U								
15	16	17	18	19	20	21	22	23	24	25	26

___ ___ ___ ___

16 24 7 24

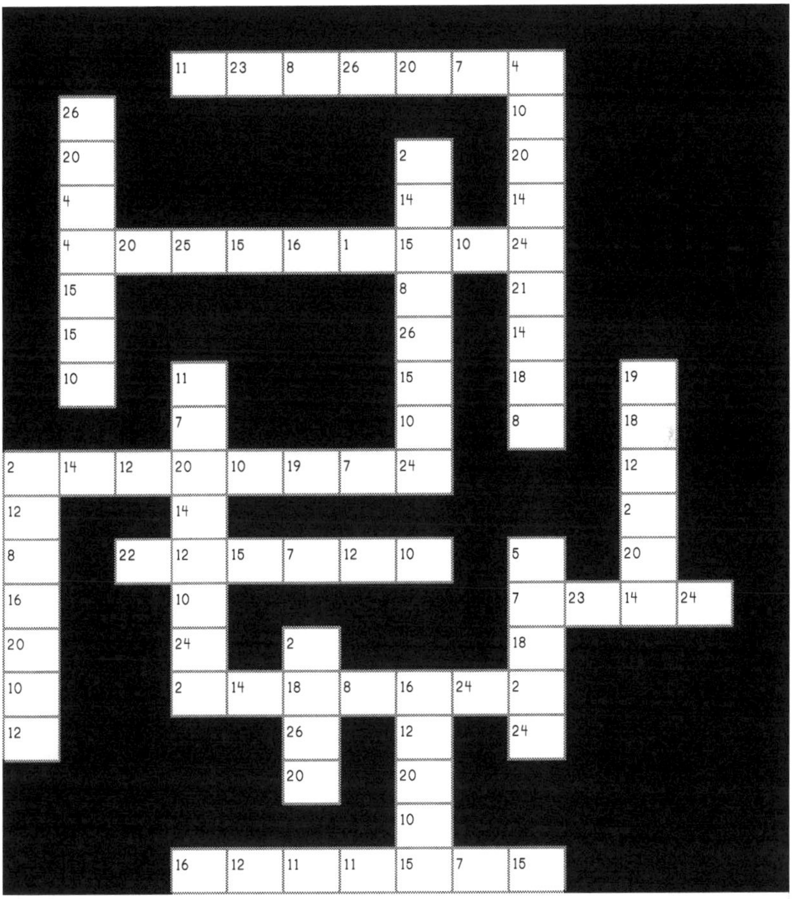

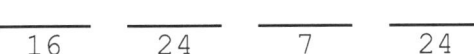

THE GODDESS

Puzzle 68: Cryptogram ㉒

```
UQI   OFYEVT   FENDPIW.
UQI   PHJH   DIOSVW   UY   GPYL.
UQSW   WQSIPT   JYPRHVY   NHB
DI   BYEVO   DEU   TY   VYU   DI
GYYPIT.
SU   SW   UQI   BYEVOIWU
HRUSJI   JYPRHVY   SV
QHLHSS.
```

WHAT IS THE NAME OF THIS PLACE?

_____

THE GODDESS

Puzzle 69: Codebreaker 36

		S			H								
1	2	3	4	5	6	7	8	9	10	11	12	13	14

									E		
15	16	17	18	19	20	21	22	23	24	25	26

___ ___ ___ ___ ___ ___

16 5 21 5 1 5

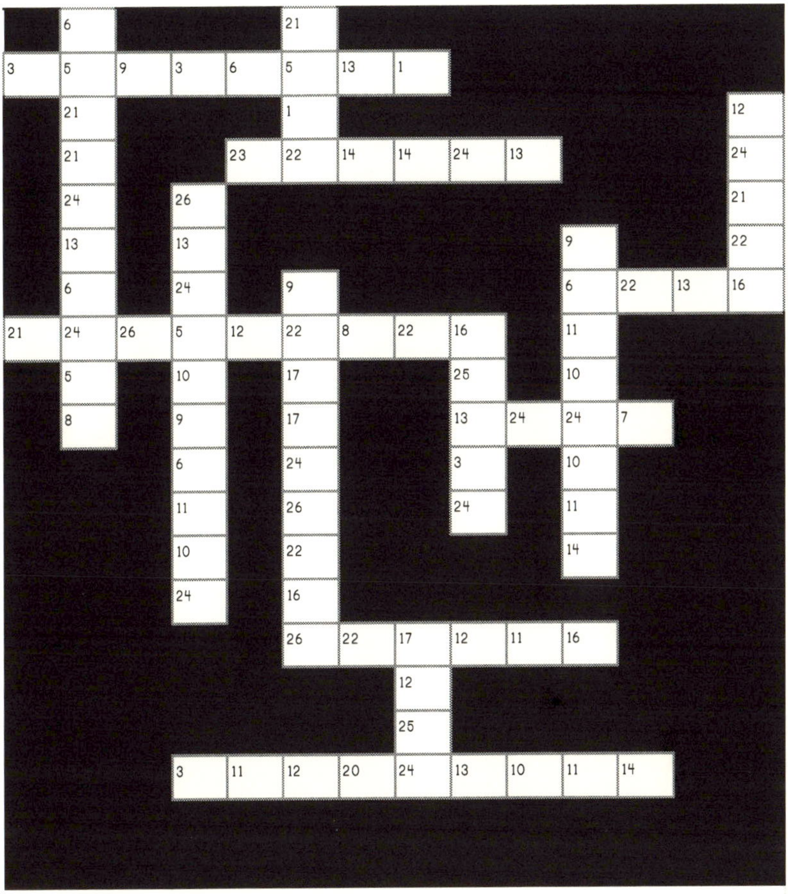

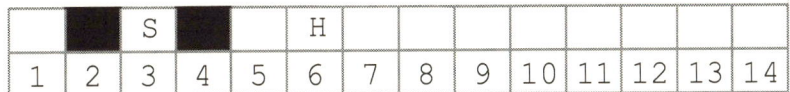

THE GODDESS

Puzzle 70: Cryptogram 92

XAY XPHX PZ SXK SVOOKZS

QABGSVPG PG SXK YATOJ?

SXVS JKIKGJZ AG XAY LAB

QKVZBTK PS.

AG VG PZOVGJ, RVT VYVL,

OPKZ SXK TKVO YPGGKT PG

SXK RATQ AR V JATQVGS

WAOEVGA.

PR LAB QKVZBTK SXPZ

QABGSVPG RTAQ CVZK SA

ZBQQPS, PS PZ SVOOKT

SXVG QABGS KWKTKZS.

WHAT IS IT'S NAME? _____

THE GODDESS

Puzzle 71: Codebreaker (160)

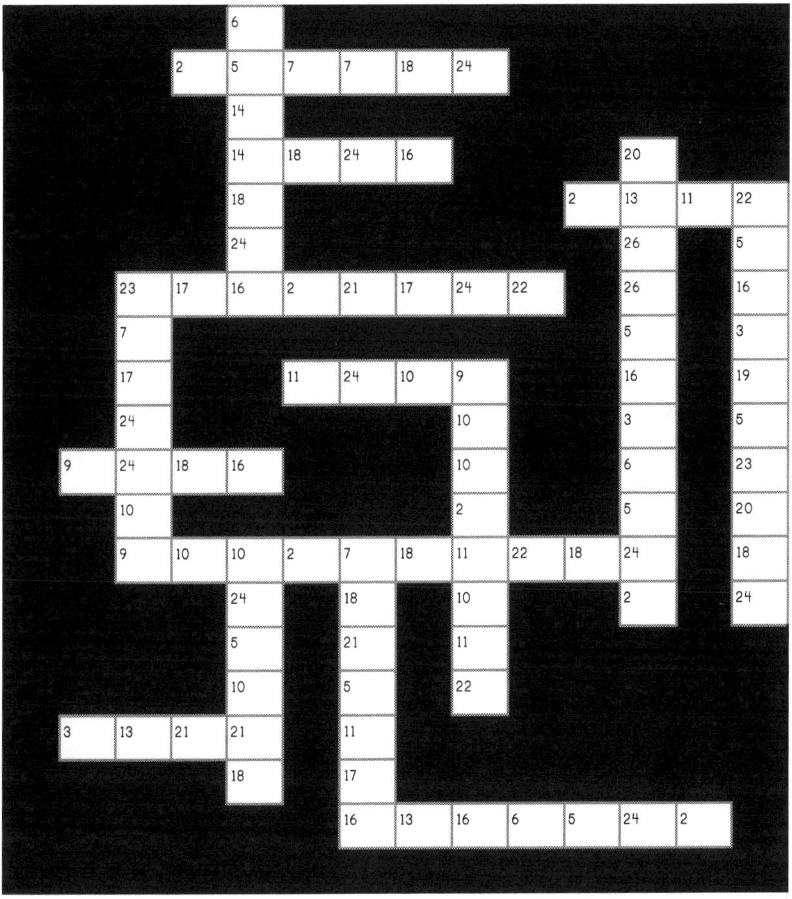

```
 ___  ___  ___  ___  ___  ___
  20   5    5   17   22   17
```

THE GODDESS

Puzzle 72: Codebreaker 145

PUZZLE WORKSHEET

This is the end of the puzzles for The Goddess. Use this space to write down clues, unscramble words, take notes, and figure out how the missing words fit into the story.

CIPHER

Congratulations on finishing the stories! Hopefully you have learned something along the way.

Have you figured out what these stories have in common? Are you ready for one final mystery? The theme of this book is printed in a cipher on the front cover. It is encrypted with a pigpen or Freemason cipher. To solve this cipher you need a keyword. Use the answer to Puzzle 67 as the key.

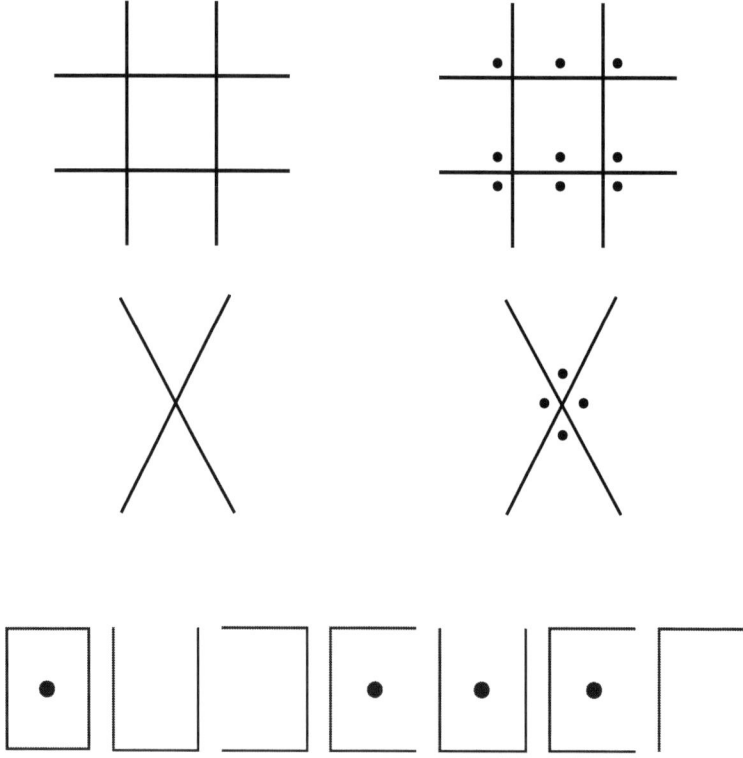

Not sure how to solve the cipher? Go to this link and we will show you:

www.mythsandlegendsbook.com/book1cipher

CLOSING

Congratulations!

Thank you for being part of Myths & Legends. We hope that you enjoyed the stories and puzzles.

We would love to hear what you thought about the book. Please leave us feedback at:

www.mythsandlegendsbook.com/feedback

Also, please leave us a review on Amazon. We are a small family business and reviews really help our books get noticed. We want everyone to have fun and be part of this journey!

Keep an eye out for Volume 2. It will be released later in 2019.

If you would like to see our other books you can find us at:

facebook.com/initiationbook

initiationbook.com

mythsandlegendsbook.com

puzzlepause.com

Thanks again and don't forget to tell us what you think. We'd love to hear from you!

- Brooklynn

OTHER PRODUCTS FROM PUZZLEPAUSE:

Initiation: An Interactive Mystery

A new way of solving popular puzzles - are you up for the challenge?

Packed with over 140 puzzles, Initiation combines the best of paper and screen. Using a secret website, you will unlock hidden clues that will help you on your journey.
Solve eleven different types of puzzles and ciphers!

SAMPLE PAGES FROM INITIATION:

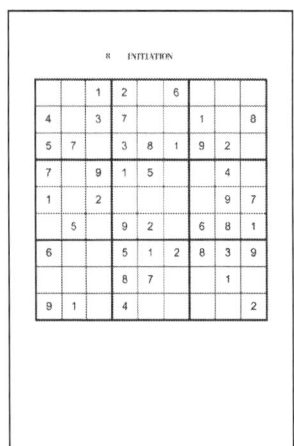
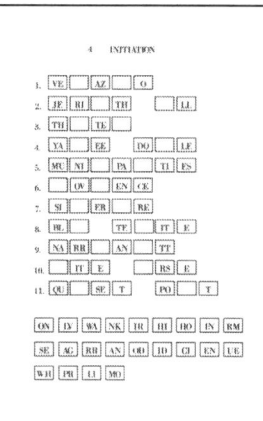
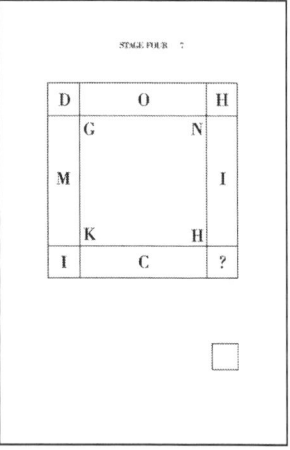

FIND ALL OF THESE GREAT BOOKS AT WWW.PUZZLEPAUSE.COM
AND ON AMAZON

AND BRAND NEW:

102 Famous Women Word Search Book

Each puzzle is based on a different woman and her accomplishments. Use the words in the puzzle and the clues in the title to figure out who she is.

From scientist to royalty, and adventurers to pioneers, these women have enriched our lives. **How many do you know?**

POCKET WORD SEARCH & SUDOKU BOOKS (5X8):

WORD SEARCH BOOKS FOR ANIMAL LOVERS:

Made in the USA
Columbia, SC
21 July 2019